Simenon, Georges, pseud.
The rich man. Translated by Jean Stewart. N.Y., Harcourt [c1971]
183 p.

t

THE
RICH
MAN

THE
RICH
MAN

GEORGES
SIMENON

Translated by Jean Stewart

A HELEN AND KURT WOLFF BOOK
HARCOURT BRACE JOVANOVICH, INC.
NEW YORK

Originally published in
French under the title
Le Riche Homme

ISBN 0–15–177162–6
Library of Congress Catalog
Card Number: 76–151139
Printed in the United States of
America
A B C D E

THE
RICH
MAN

He drew up the truck, loaded with hampers of mussels, outside the bistrot, over the front of which the words *Chez Mimile* were inscribed in yellow letters.

Doudou the deaf-mute climbed out at the same time as himself, by the other door, and followed him, gliding noiselessly, barefoot, his blue cotton trousers rolled up high as usual.

Victor Lecoin was tall and powerfully built, broad-shouldered and deep-chested. His rubber waders, turned over at the top, looked like musketeers' boots, and he was wearing his everlasting black leather jacket. He was conscious of his strength. When he turned the handle and opened the door he felt as though he were filling up the whole doorway, and in the little café where four men sat playing cards by the window he was like a giant among dwarfs.

He raised one hand toward them and muttered a vague greeting.

Mimile, mechanically, ran a cloth over the old-fashioned zinc counter and called out:

"Morning, Chief. . . ."

Everyone called him that, for he towered over them not only with his great height but with his money.

Doudou had come in close behind him and had gone to lean on the other end of the counter.

Mimile, in shirt sleeves and black waistcoat, wearing his faded blue apron by way of uniform, set a bottle of white wine and a glass on the counter in front of Lecoin, as he did every day.

Doudou, however, drank neither wine nor spirits, he did not smoke, and he had never been seen with a girl. Mimile poured him some lemonade with a dash of grenadine, as if he were a child.

Lecoin might have gone straight home on leaving the mussel beds, for he always had a cask of wine broached and his own was better than the bistrot's. But this halt was an old habit. It helped to make him feel strong and assert his superiority, if not his sway, over other men.

Standing in front of the bar he seemed taller, broader, heavier than ever. He spoke little, and never gesticulated, even when communicating with Doudou, for whom a glance was enough. He rolled a cigarette between his thick fingers, staring vaguely at the card players, who were the same four every day.

Théo Porchet was there, and Jo Chevalier, Louis Cardis, and Marcel Lefranc, whom everyone in the village called little Marcel.

Théo was a little man too, thin and puny, with a perpetual sneering grin on his face. He was the village clown and he was proud of his reputation.

He kept darting timid and yet insolent glances at Lecoin. He was a dealer in hardware. He kept a shop on the church square, almost opposite the grocer's, and he sold a bit of everything, minor electrical equipment, kerosene, storm lamps, ropes, and for over a year a washing machine had stood proudly in his shop window.

Lecoin had immediately noticed that the little man was excited and kept watching him stealthily.

"Say, you fellows, I've got an idea we're going to have a good laugh by and by."

He was sniggering, watching the others, who avoided smiling too openly.

Lecoin knit his thick, bushy eyebrows. He could not understand the hardware dealer's remark and wondered what it might refer to. It must have been something funny, since Jo Chevalier, who was a mussel gatherer and had sold him six hampers of mussels only an hour previously, was making an effort not to burst out laughing.

"Have you seen her?" Jo asked.

"She got off the bus at twenty past eight, with a bundle no bigger than a handbag."

"Is she a good-looker?"

Lecoin felt ill at ease. He realized that he was the target of their hints, their rather fearful glances.

The walls were painted yellow and hung with colored advertisements and, framed in black, the Law on Public Intoxication. In the kitchen, the door of which was ajar, its glass panes partly veiled by a net curtain, Mimile's wife was at work, her heavy breasts swinging.

"She doesn't need to be good-looking. . . ."

This time they laughed out loud and Lecoin felt himself even more their butt. Apart from Théo, however, they seemed constrained and uneasy.

"She wears a skirt. . . . Isn't that enough? . . ."

And Théo stared almost brazenly at Lecoin, with a mocking grin on his big mouth. Then Lecoin noticed a movement behind him and saw the deaf-mute moving forward noiselessly, with no expression on his face. His huge hands were wide open as if to grasp the hardware dealer's skinny throat.

He, too, had understood. He was used to watching people's lips, and although he could not hear, he was supposed to be the scandalmonger of the village, for he knew about everything that happened there.

Lecoin looked at him and lifted his hand, and for once the deaf-mute seemed reluctant to obey. Merely seeing him draw near, Théo shrank back on his seat and the

6

others assumed an absent-minded air. Mimile hastily broke the silence:

"What d'you think of this batch?" he asked, pointing to the bottle. "I got it from François. . . ."

Lecoin did not bother to answer him. Something must have happened to give Théo the courage to brave him, and he wondered what it could be. Now, because of the three or four steps Doudou had taken toward them, the card players had fallen silent and the only remarks to be heard were:

"Three."

"Of what?"

"Jacks."

"Mine are kings. *Belote* . . ."

This relaxed the atmosphere a little, but Doudou still glowered, and it was with the reluctance of a big dog forcibly restrained from attacking that he had gone back to his place at the far end of the bar.

The clock (it, too, was an advertisement) showed twelve o'clock, which meant that it was a quarter to. Low tide had been at nine, and although it was not a spring tide almost everyone had been to the mussel beds; Lecoin, with Doudou's help, had filled five hampers.

He not only had his own mussel beds like the other men, but he bought their produce from them. He went farther afield than Marsilly, working with people from Esnandes and Marans. He had two trucks to take his mussels in to La Rochelle.

In order to assert his authority, he went on watching the card players, seemingly calm and somewhat contemptuous. Then he flung some coins down on the counter and moved toward the door, without anyone's daring to smile again. Doudou followed him, and his attitude made it clear that he was sorry he had not been allowed to crush Théo.

Lecoin was not mayor of the village. He was not even on the municipal council, but he was the important man, the rich man, and everyone accepted his authority.

So Théo's sneer, the mysterious words he had uttered, were all the more unexpected. True, the hardware dealer made fun of everyone, and he was allowed to do so because he was ugly and sickly, with a crooked face twisted in a bitter grin. It was his wife Eugénie who looked after the shop, while he spent most of his time playing cards, when he could find partners.

Today, for the first time, he had attacked Lecoin, who was still trying to understand why. Had the little man really been trying to provoke him? Was he tipsy enough already, at a quarter to twelve, to throw prudence to the winds?

Lecoin climbed into the driver's seat of his truck and Doudou automatically got in beside him. He had only a hundred yards to go to the church square and another hundred along the Esnandes road to reach his place.

He drove the truck through the gateway and into the huge garage which housed the second truck, the machine for washing the mussels, and a Peugeot car.

As usual, he went in by the kitchen door, and he stopped short on the threshold, surprised to see before him a girl he did not know. She stared back at him, curiously. She must have guessed he was the master of the house, but his hip boots, his broad shoulders, his strongly marked features did not seem to impress her.

She was a lanky child with long thin legs, wearing a black cotton dress shiny with wear, which had been washed so often that it barely reached her knees.

Her bosom was scarcely formed and her face was neither pretty nor actually plain.

"Morning," she said at last.

"Morning."

He added, after a pause:

"What's your name?"

"Alice. . . ."

"How old are you? Fifteen?"

"Sixteen."

He shrugged his shoulders and went through into the wide passage where the coatrack stood. He pulled off his boots and his leather jacket, keeping on his blue seaman's jersey. He opened the door into the office that overlooked the courtyard, where his wife Jeanne was dealing with invoices.

At last he sat down heavily on the opposite side of the office and began rolling a cigarette.

"How many hampers?"

"About forty."

"Weren't the stakes damaged by the last couple of days' wind?"

"Nothing's shifted. . . . Who's that girl in the kitchen?"

"The new maid. You know Louise has gone off to Niort, to get married."

He knew and he didn't know. Such things did not concern him and he only listened to them with half an ear.

He was equally unconcerned about the purchase and sale of mussels. That was Jeanne's department; she was a former schoolteacher, and good at accounts.

"Where does she come from?"

"The National Assistance Home."

"D'you mean she's never worked in a private house?"

"She's worked at a farm, near Surgères. . . ."

He grumbled: "It's that one, is it?"

"What does that matter to us?"

It had been the talk of the whole province, even though the authorities had decided there was no case for prosecution.

Alice, after having been brought up in a National Assistance home, had been put in service with the Paquots, farmers in the neighborhood of Surgères, in a hamlet of a few houses. This must have been rather less than a year ago. Paquot was an illiterate brute, obese and greasy, with little piggish eyes. It was astonishing that so decent a woman as his wife had been willing to marry him.

He must have been about fifty. He had an only child, a

girl, who was a boarder in a convent school at La Rochelle.

No one knew exactly what had happened. But a neighbor had gone to the police.

"There are things going on at the Paquots'."

"What d'you mean by things?"

"Things, you know. When Mme Paquot goes in to Surgères or La Rochelle her husband takes advantage of it."

"To do what?"

"To have a bit of fun with the maid."

"He's entitled to, isn't he, provided she's willing?"

"She's not yet sixteen and she comes from the orphanage."

"How d'you know he has what you call fun with her?"

"I've guessed as much for some time. He's always been one for the girls. But this one's a bit young."

"Are you lodging a complaint?"

"No, seeing it's not my business, but in our village we're all disgusted."

"What's the girl's name?"

"Alice."

"Alice what?"

"Just Alice. I don't think she's ever known her father or mother. One day last week I went over to Paquot's to borrow his tractor, because mine's being repaired. There was nobody around the house or in the fields. I knocked at the front door and nobody answered. So I went in, naturally. I went through the room they use as a parlor, and in the kitchen I caught them at it."

"Making love?"

"I wouldn't quite say that. Nearly. Paquot had lifted up the girl's dress and had his hand you know where. He had his fly open and everything was sticking out."

The police had made a brief inquiry. They had questioned Alice, who had replied in monosyllables.

"Did he rape you?"

"No."

"Did you let him do it to you?"

"Yes and no."

"What d'you mean by that?"

"Not everything."

"Did he fondle you?"

"Yes."

"And you?"

"He used to put it in my hand."

"Often?"

"About a dozen times, when his wife went to La Rochelle."

"Did you never complain?"

"No."

"Why not?"

"Because I suppose all men are like that."

The matter had been discussed before the magistrate.

Paquot had been summoned; he swore the girl had enticed him.

"I never tried to go any further. And now, on account of that bitch, my wife won't speak to me."

Jeanne Lecoin was a woman of about fifty, three years older than her husband. She had grown rather stout, and her hard-featured face was always pale. The fact was that she hardly ever went out of the house and spent most of her time in the office.

"I suppose you're not afraid?"

"Of what?"

"Of being tempted yourself."

Lecoin reddened involuntarily.

"I've never gone in for little girls. Can she do her job?"

"It's easy for her, since I do all the cooking."

Presently they went into the dining room, and Alice served the meal, clumsily. Lecoin avoided looking at her, though he could not have said why. In any case, there was nothing attractive about her. She was a thin, straight stick of a girl, with a nondescript face and dark hair hanging lankly on either side of her face.

They had grilled ham with potatoes and cabbage from the garden, with apples and pears after, also grown on the property.

Theirs was the largest and finest house in the village. It was about two hundred years old and for a long time had belonged to an aristocratic family. The last occupant, Charles de Rosy, was an old bachelor who had tried to restore the family fortunes by gambling on the Stock Exchange, where he had finally lost all his money.

When the house and land were put up for auction Lecoin had got them.

Forty years earlier the best lands and most of the farms at Marsilly had belonged to the Rosy family. It was here that Victor Lecoin had been born, for his father was then a laborer on one of these farms.

Now the stone house that some people called the château was his home, and he owned the principal farm, as well as pieces of land here and there.

Doudou did not eat in the house. They had tried to persuade him, but he had always refused. He lived in a kind of hut at the far end of the courtyard, a few yards from the garage, and prepared his own meals. He would eat anything, so people said, even rooks.

He had been born in the neighborhood. His mother was Fernande, a drunken slut who had no husband and whom men visited when they were drunk. She was dirty and no longer young, and she lived in a hovel close to the seashore.

She died when Doudou was only twelve, and the Lecoins had adopted him to save him from being shut up in an institution.

He was strong, stronger than Lecoin, but he never did any harm to anyone. He had a huge head, with pale blue eyes and a flat nose. His arms were very long and his hands were capable of crushing anything.

"Are you going to Marans?"

"I'll go there with the other truck as soon as I've

finished eating. The whole load has to be at La Rochelle before five."

The dining room was big and high-ceilinged, like all the rooms in the house. It opened straight into the kitchen, from which came savory smells mingled with the smell of furniture polish.

Between Lecoin and his wife there was no bond of feeling, only the habit of living together. They each had their own job, and apart from mussels and oysters they had little to talk about to one another.

"Will you be back early?"

"I don't know."

Now and then, about once a week, he did not come home until ten at night, and on these occasions he was half tipsy. These were the days when, as he put it, he went on a spree.

Today, Friday, he did not know whether or not he wanted to go on a spree. He'd decide that later.

Doudou was busy washing the mussels. It was early March and the sky was that lavender-blue characteristic of the La Rochelle region. The air was mild. The first bee of the season was buzzing around the dining room, and that morning, above the mussel beds, there had only been a couple of tiny clouds lazily floating like balloons.

Lecoin involuntarily kept glancing at Alice, and he felt slightly ill at ease.

As the mussels were washed, Doudou's job was to collect them, weigh the hampers, fasten the lids, and hoist

15

them into the truck. At the same time, in the office, Jeanne Lecoin wrote the names and addresses of the consignees on yellow labels.

Lecoin, meanwhile, had taken the second truck and driven to Charron, a village with low-built houses, amid marshes that were already typical of the Vendée. He only collected some twenty hampers, for he met with competition here, and many mussel pickers had their own trucks.

He did not fail to look in at the bar, so as to show himself and make his presence felt, and instead of one table of card players there were two.

"Hello, Chief."

Here, too, he was "the Chief," the important man. He drank a glass of white wine and rolled himself a cigarette, then got back to Marsilly in time to wash the mussels, fasten the hampers, and hoist them into the first truck, which held the whole load.

Doudou did not accompany him to La Rochelle. He drove there by himself. Today his thoughts involuntarily dwelt on Alice, who had seemed to be naked under her dress of black glazed cotton. From the way that dress hung on her skinny body he'd have sworn that she wore nothing underneath it, not even panties.

And then he recalled the stories he had been told, about how fat, sweating Paquot had lifted her dress and fondled her while he put his penis into her hand.

It was unhealthy. He was annoyed with himself for thinking of such things. The girl was not good-looking and she seemed dirty. There was no bath on the attic floor where she had her bedroom, only a big washtub.

He turned left in front of the station and drove quickly into the yard, close to the raised platform that was used for loading and unloading. He had to visit the sanitary inspector, who sat in a sort of glass cage.

"Hello, Lecoin."

No "Chief" for him from this self-important functionary.

"How many hampers?"

"Sixty-two."

"All from Marsilly?"

"Twenty-two from Charron."

He patiently filled in the sanitary inspector's forms, which had to accompany each of the hampers.

"All for France?"

"No. There are some for Switzerland and about twenty for Algeria."

He rolled another cigarette while he unloaded the hampers from the truck and laid them out in the fast-shipment hall, close to the weighing machine.

When he had all his forms he put them in place on top of each hamper and the official in charge of dispatch came up.

"Hello, Chief."

He was the boss again.

"Have you weighed them?"

"Yes. They're all right."

"I'll just check a few of them, for form's sake."

17

Lecoin handed him a ten-franc tip, and took the sheet of paper to hand in at the desk.

They had known him there for a long time. He knew all the staff and addressed them indiscriminately as Toto.

"Well, Toto, how's the fishing?"

For the cashier went angling in the Marans canal.

"Not sensational, but I can't complain. Eels, of course."

The canal was an unused one with at least two feet of mud at the bottom.

He drew an enormous wallet from the pocket of his leather jacket, for he paid for everything in cash, as cattle dealers do. His wallet was worn at the edges and the seams had split in several places. It never occurred to him to buy another; not out of meanness, but because he didn't care.

There was a tip for the cashier too.

"Thanks, Chief. You're coming tomorrow?"

"If we pick up enough mussels."

Low tide would be an hour later, about ten in the morning. It would be possible to start work in the front mussel beds by eight, when the sea had uncovered them. There would also be an opportunity to tidy up the oyster beds.

He thrust his wallet into his pocket and climbed back into his truck. He drove along the quayside, passed in front of the big clock, and parked a little farther on.

He walked about a hundred yards and went into a bar called The Sailor's Rest.

"Hello, Victor!" called out the woman standing behind the bar. "It's quite a while since we've seen you."

This was the only place where he was known as Victor. Even his wife had formed the habit of calling him by his surname; she would say: "Morning, Lecoin."

Nénette was more familiar. She was a chunky little woman of about forty-five who had retained her youthful freshness. He had known her when she was still a streetwalker, some ten years earlier. And from time to time, when nobody else there attracted him, he would go upstairs with her.

The bar was deep and narrow and at this time of day there were hardly ever any customers. In any case, Nénette liked that better. One at a time. Particularly when they were like Lecoin.

"What d'you want?"

He looked in the mirror behind the bottles, eying two girls perched on high stools and watching him. He did not remember either of them.

One of the two was a buxom girl with a naïve expression and a foolish smile. The other, a brunette, was pretending to make up her face, holding her handbag in her left hand and glancing into the mirror it contained.

"Is that all you've got?"

"I've got a terrific girl that you don't know. She's barely been at it for a month. She's at home, just down the road. Shall I get her for you?"

"Yes."

As soon as Nénette had left, the dark girl moved to a nearer stool and murmured to him:

"D'you come here often, dearie?"

"For one thing I'm not your dearie. For another, whether I come often or not is my own business."

He enjoyed being surly; it seemed to do him good.

"You know, I didn't mean to say . . . You don't look mean, though. . . ."

He shrugged his shoulders, went around the counter, and poured himself a brandy, while the two girls watched him with some surprise. Then he went back to sit down, with the glass in front of him.

"Aren't you going to treat us?"

"When Nénette's come back."

The blonde was now sprucing herself up. Before five minutes had elapsed Nénette returned.

"She'll be here in a minute. Just think, I found her asleep. She's going to have a quick shower. . . . Will you stand us a round?"

He shrugged his shoulders. Why not? This was the way it always happened.

"Have you got any champagne on ice?"

"I've always got champagne on ice. I see you've helped yourself; that's right."

Then, addressing him as well as the two girls, she proposed:

"Why don't we go and sit in the back room?"

A door at the end of the barroom was half hidden by a dark red draped curtain, beyond which one could glimpse a more intimate room with a large sofa, also red, some armchairs, and a table in the center.

"Can we?" the blonde asked, looking at him.

He nodded and tossed off his glass.

"Pour me another."

He needed to get himself into the mood. Outside, the old stones of the two towers on either side of the harbor entry were flushed by the rays of the setting sun.

Nénette went to get a bottle from the refrigerator, and the four of them sat down in the little parlor. The table was covered with an old-fashioned fringed cloth.

"What's new, Victor?"

"Nothing."

"Here's to you, and to these nice girls too. Lucky for you they happened to be here."

The new girl now came in; she was somewhat younger and wore a very short skirt. She exclaimed:

"Oh, what a shame to start without me. What's your name?"

"Victor."

"Well, Victor love, you're a strapping fellow. I bet people don't often pick a quarrel with you. Can I feel?"

She felt his biceps and gave an admiring whistle.

"Say, are you going to give all four of us a good time?"

They emptied their glasses. So did he, and Nénette

went to the next room to get another bottle. The new girl, whose name was Lucie, was perched on the sofa in a position that showed a great deal of her legs.

Not until the third round did the atmosphere liven up. Lecoin fondled the girls in turn, sometimes two at a time. He was drinking hard, and they saw to it that his glass was never empty.

"Say, Nénette . . ."

She hurried up.

"Can we go upstairs?"

"You know what a risk I run, don't you? They've been very strict, lately. Still, I'll make an exception for you. Here's the key to my room. Are you taking all three of them?"

"You can bring us up something to drink."

The staircase was dark and winding. He knew it as well as he knew Nénette's room with its big walnut bedstead, doilies everywhere, and an incredible number of knicknacks, like the prizes at a fair.

"What shall we do now?"

"You can get undressed, to begin with."

This to the newcomer. The other two were about to do the same.

"Wait till I tell you."

Nénette brought up a bottle and some glasses. Half an hour later, she brought up champagne for the fourth time and found the three women stark naked.

"We only need you now," Lecoin told her.

"I have to stay downstairs. I've got two customers."

Lecoin was slightly tipsy, but he still had all his wits about him. He was trying hard to enjoy himself, to make jokes. The three girls made clumsy attempts to help him.

"Who'll you start with?"

"You, since you've asked for it."

"Aren't you going to undress?"

"No."

The pale green silk curtains were drawn in front of the windows and there was a pink shade over the ceiling lamp. Steps and voices sounded on the sidewalk outside, where everyday life was going on. Sometimes a boat returning to port sounded its siren. The tide was high and the trawlers were coming back one after the other.

In fact, he felt no desire for any of the three women, but since he was there he had to go through with it.

"D'you come often?"

"Yes."

"D'you always take three?"

"I take whatever's there."

He took another of the girls, the little plump one, and came almost immediately.

"Hi! Drink up."

He had left his glass empty and he was offered it full. They imagined their trick had taken him in, but he was well aware that they were trying to make him drunk.

This went on until eight o'clock, and when he went downstairs again he had to watch the steps carefully.

"Was it all right?"

"Sure."

"Were the girls nice?"

"They did what they could. What do I owe you?"

"Seven bottles of wine and two brandies. . . ."

She did her reckoning on a scrap of paper, which she pushed toward him. He drew the thick wallet from his pocket.

"You're always well heeled!" she commented.

That pleased him. He needed to assert his superiority somehow, and his stature and strength were not enough. After all, Doudou was just as strong or stronger, and he was only a half-wit.

"Aren't you hungry?"

"I'll have something to eat when I get home."

"Shall we see you again soon, Victor?"

"Maybe. . . ."

But not until the fancy took him. When he went out, night had fallen and the street lamps were lit. Before climbing into his truck, he walked across the quay and stood for a while by the water's edge, watching the little fishing boats rocking below him.

The sea heaved gently up and down like the breast of a sleeper, but there were no real waves, and the harbor lights were reflected to infinity.

When he was about sixteen or seventeen he had thought of becoming a fisherman. But everyone at Marsilly went in for mussel breeding or farming, often both at once. He had done the same and had had no cause for complaint.

There was a brightly lit café close to the Big Clock,

and the weather was so mild that the windows stood wide open, just as in the summertime when the terrace was thronged with people.

He felt like sitting there for a drink. He could not decide what to order and finally muttered:

"A brandy."

Usually he drank about two bottles of wine a day, sometimes three when the weather was very hot, and it did not have the slightest effect on him.

When he was on a spree, like today, he took no count of glasses or bottles. There was a restaurant on the first floor. Here, too, people could be seen playing cards, but they weren't the same sort as at Marsilly or Charron. These were office workers or tradespeople. They were playing bridge, and the proprietor, napkin in hand, was standing behind one of the players to watch the game.

As his eyes roamed around the café he noticed a young woman sitting by herself before a glass of vermouth. He had never seen her before. In her prim tailormade suit she looked like a respectable little bourgeoise waiting for her husband.

He was surprised when she stared back at him, and averted his gaze. When he looked at her again he had the impression that she was discreetly smiling at him.

She was much more attractive than the three girls at Nénette's, and he regretted the way he had spent the evening. She wore a pleated white blouse that emphasized the youth and freshness of her face.

He could not very well go up and join her at her table,

but he was convinced, now, that she was smiling at him encouragingly. He jerked his head toward the quayside to let her know he would wait for her there.

He paid and went out, away from the bright lights of the café which shone over a wide stretch of pavement. Three minutes later she came out too, and looked around for him.

"Here I am."

"Oh, good! I wasn't sure I'd understood you right. . . . Where shall we go?"

"D'you know a hotel?"

"I'm a stranger here."

"Are you passing through?"

"I've come from Paris to see my mother at the hospital."

"Is she seriously ill?"

"No. A nurse."

He moved toward the Porte de la Grosse Horloge and she took his arm quite naturally.

"I know a small hotel, to the left," Lecoin said, "where they won't ask us any questions."

"No. 7, Monsieur Victor."

"What would you like to drink?"

"I'm not particularly thirsty."

"Champagne?"

"Yes, that would be fine."

"Send us up a bottle of champagne."

"Yes, Monsieur Victor."

To some he was "the Chief," *le patron;* to others,

Monsieur Victor; to his wife, Lecoin, and to Nénette, just Victor.

He felt sorry he had used up most of his strength, but he banked on his native vigor.

"Do you ever come to Paris?"

"About once a year, or every two years."

"Where do you stay?"

"Always near the Gare Montparnasse."

"I live on the Rue Vavin. It's not far off."

She looked like a respectable young lady rather than a prostitute. He felt shy with her. He had not even touched her by the time their drinks were brought up.

"And what about you? D'you live at La Rochelle?"

"At Marsilly."

"You're the skipper of a fishing boat."

She was misled by the seaman's cap that he wore, like most of those in his trade.

"I breed mussels," he said, as though joking.

"You're kidding me, aren't you?"

"Not at all. It's the strict truth. You drive stakes into the sea where the shore is uncovered at low tide. Between them you fix nets. Then you only have to collect spat out at sea and fasten it to these nets and stakes."

"What's spat?"

"Tiny mussels stuck together. You go and look at them from time to time and shift them if need be, and remove crabs and starfish. After a year they'll have grown fairly big, and some people sell them then. They are finer still after two years, and even fatter after three."

27

"Your good health."

"And yours. Are you stopping long in La Rochelle?"

"I'm leaving tomorrow. In an hour I'm going to meet my mother when she comes off duty."

"Pity."

"Why?"

"Because we might have become good friends. D'you come often?"

"About once every six months."

"Next time, drop me a line."

He pulled a notebook from his pocket and wrote down his address.

"Won't your wife mind?"

"No."

"Isn't she jealous?"

"No."

"You're certainly lucky! Are you sure it won't upset her?"

"Quite sure."

"Shall I take my things off?"

He undressed her himself, but only partly, so that the affair might seem casual.

He stayed with her a long time, talking, which was unusual for him. To explain his lukewarm ardor he told her about the three girls at Nénette's, and as he expected she looked at him with admiration.

"Well, you're a prize winner, all right!"

She did not say *tu;* she had not once called him darling. He found it hard to place her, and when they had emptied the bottle he had to make an effort to pull out his wallet. He took a number of notes and went over to thrust them into her handbag. She watched him, but made no protest.

"Will you write to me?"

"I promise."

"Well, see you in six months."

He was slightly unsteady, but none the less he drove his truck safely home and into the garage. The light was on in Doudou's hut. In the house, too. It was only nine o'clock. He went in by the kitchen door as usual. His wife was showing Alice where to put away the dishes and cutlery.

"Have you had dinner?" she asked him.

"No, but it doesn't matter."

"There was some fish this evening, but warmed-up fish isn't nice. What would you like to eat? You had ham at midday. . . ."

"Some bread and cheese, I think. . . . And a drop of white wine. . . ."

She did not stare at him to try to guess where he had been or what he had been doing. As he had said, his escapades left her unmoved.

Had there ever been love between them? Perhaps right at the beginning, when she was twenty-eight and he twenty-five. He had rented a farm, "The Four Winds," which he still owned today and had leased to his brother. At the time it had belonged to Charles de Rosy, whose solid mansion they now occupied.

Jeanne had been a schoolteacher, and he had left school at thirteen.

What was it about her that had impressed him? And why had she agreed to marry him? Had she felt his strength, his will to succeed?

She had helped him, she still helped him to the best of her ability, but their intimacy went no further. In short, they had accepted nothing more of marriage than the big double bed in which they lay apart.

They were just associates.

CHAPTER 2

He got up at half past five the next morning, as he had done all his life, summer and winter alike. When he had been a farm hand he used to rise even earlier, for electric milking machines had been unknown and the cows had to be milked at half past four in the morning.

There was an empty place in the bed beside him. Jeanne was up already, and he could hear her going to and fro downstairs.

He went into the bathroom, and had a shower and a shave. He was not one of those men who shave every other day or even only once a week, on a Saturday.

The bedroom, like the rest of the house, was furnished

with old-fashioned pieces of furniture, chiefly of the Louis-Philippe period, heavy, massive wooden articles which had almost all been bought at auction sales.

The night before, he had found it difficult to get to sleep. He had listened to his wife's regular breathing, with an occasional hissing intake of breath. Immediately above them, Alice, too, must have been asleep.

Was anyone in the house really happy? If he had not been slightly drunk he would not have asked himself the question. Jeanne, in particular—was she happy?

She never grumbled. Her face was neutral, expressionless. She worked from morning till night and never went out except to shop in La Rochelle about once a month.

What did she think about, alone all day? And why had she married him?

When he woke, the aftertaste of these thoughts was still with him. He had no hangover. The morning after his worst drinking bouts he was always as fresh as ever.

He dressed and went down to the dining room, where his place was set. The kitchen door was open and he saw Jeanne showing Alice what to do. The maid was wearing the same black dress as the day before, probably her only one; her hair was untidy, and she looked a little pale from having risen so early.

Once again there sprang into his mind the picture of this child and that brute Paquot shamelessly taking advantage of her.

"Morning, Lecoin."

"Morning, Jeanne."

Alice set before him a bowl of soup, made yesterday and reheated. It was his habit, every morning, to have a full meal, with bacon and eggs, then cheese, and perhaps a little fruit to finish with. In the winter he sometimes had a big plate of chestnuts with coarse bread and butter.

Outside, it was still dark. He finally rolled himself a cigarette and then got up and put on his boots, his black leather jacket, and his seaman's cap. This had become a kind of uniform for him, which he only varied slightly when he had to go to town.

His one pleasant memory of the previous day was that of the young woman he had met in the café, whom he would have liked to see again. He had given her his address, written on a scrap of paper. Would she really get in touch with him the next time she came to La Rochelle? What was she, in Paris? A streetwalker? He found that hard to believe. She would surely not have kept so fresh.

His thoughts were somewhat confused; so, too, were his impressions. He recalled his first meeting with his wife, during a village fête at Nieul. The dance floor was in the center of a huge tent; she sat there alone, and nobody asked her to dance. Not that she was any less attractive than other girls, but the fact that she was the schoolmistress intimidated the young men.

She was sitting on one of the benches that stood all around the tent, with her hands on her knees and an expressionless face, watching the others dance.

"May I have the pleasure of this dance?"

He had said it almost defiantly, convinced that she would refuse.

But she had simply stood up and followed him. She danced rather stiffly, as though on the defensive. He did not know what to say to her. He had still been very gauche at that time.

"Are you coming to the fête at Marsilly too? It's in a month."

He had taken her back to her seat.

"What can I get you from the buffet?"

"A glass of lemonade, if they have any."

He had been twenty-two then. He was not used to such formality with girls.

"Are you from these parts?"

"From Bressuire, in Deux-Sèvres."

"You're not country-born?"

"My father sells fertilizers."

He had left her side for fear of embarrassing her, but he had not danced with any other girls. Twice more he had sought her out. She had glanced up at him gratefully, as though he had been making some sort of sacrifice for her sake.

She had been slimmer then and her face was gentler, her body more lissome.

Had he really been in love? After so many years, it seemed strange to him. For three months, six months perhaps? He had contrived to meet her when she came out of school, and he always had a sense of inferiority.

"You know, I've had no education. I left school at thirteen and I didn't even get my diploma."

She had smiled reassuringly. For in those days she still smiled.

"Do you like your job?" he went on to ask.

"It's the only one I know."

"I suppose you wouldn't like to live on a farm?"

"Why not?"

"Because the work there is never ending. There's always something to be done."

Three months later, they were married at Bressuire. She had three sisters, who looked at him mistrustfully. The father, however, seemed to accept the situation.

They had not gone away for a honeymoon. The farm was waiting for them, and Jeanne had immediately been plunged into its routine.

Had there actually been any honeymoon? He had been impressed to find that she was a virgin. He had tried not to behave brutally, but in the months that followed he came to realize that she did not respond to his lovemaking. With patient docility, she submitted to it. After a year she was still childless, and he had to resign himself to the idea that she could never have a child.

She played an increasingly important part on the farm, quietly and, so it seemed, tirelessly.

And there had gradually grown up that sort of association in which feelings played no part. He was fond of her, basically, but he did not love her.

35

"I'm going to see Daniel."

This was his brother, who was five years younger than himself. People said of him:

"He's the best fellow in the world."

None the less Daniel, when he was younger, had never kept the same job for more than six months. And yet he had stayed at school till he was sixteen. He had been their father's favorite. He was a good-looking fellow and as a child had had fine curly hair.

He was a weak character. He had worked at La Rochelle for a pork butcher and then taken various jobs here and there in the neighborhood.

Then he had had the good fortune to marry Véronique, who had been working at a hairdresser's on the Place d'Armes.

When Victor Lecoin bought the house he now lived in and extended his mussel beds, he had established his brother and Véronique on Four Winds Farm, which still belonged to him.

It was a big isolated building almost on the seashore, between Esnandes and Marsilly. It comprised over twenty hectares of land, and there were twenty cows in one shed, a dozen calves in another, and in one corner a magnificent bull with a ring in his nose.

He found Véronique busy fitting the electric milkers onto the cow's udders. She had not completed her toilet but was pretty none the less.

"Is Daniel here?"

"He's getting ready for the Niort fair. He intended to go and see you on the way."

Daniel enjoyed fairs, when the cafés were loud with noise and thick with pipe and cigarette smoke and the heavy reek of cheap wine. He would stay there for hours arguing with his pals, drinking glass after glass, and seldom coming home before nightfall.

Véronique was patient. She never recriminated, even if she was at heart somewhat jealous. Wasn't he her man? She would wait up for him till all hours and sometimes had to undress him and put him to bed.

In front of Victor, people kept quiet, except for that little swine Théo who had done his comic turn the day before. On the other hand everyone felt friendly toward Daniel, and he could ask anyone for help. Women found him attractive, too, and could hardly resist his invariable good humor.

For Daniel, nothing mattered, nothing was serious. Everything turned out all right in the end, didn't it?

"I'll go and see him."

As he went past the vegetable garden next to the house, he saw his father, who was now over eighty and had become more and more stooped. He looked like a hunchback but kept on working none the less.

"Hello, Father."

"Hello, son."

They seemed to belong to different races. The old man had never been tall, and he was a silent, solitary creature who for nearly twenty years had served as laborer on the same farm. He was devoid of any sort of ambition.

Had he not always considered Victor a stranger? His true son, the one with whom he had eventually chosen to live, was Daniel.

And Daniel, hearing voices, had now opened the front door.

"I was just going to see you."

"So your wife was telling me."

"Will you come in for a moment?"

"Yes. And I wouldn't say no to a glass of wine."

His brother was dressed for town. He was a whole head shorter than Victor, and his features were far more finely cut.

Logs were blazing in the big fireplace. The house was warm and pleasant. It was said to have been a monastery in the old days, and to have been connected to La Rochelle by an underground passage during the siege of that town.

In any case, carved stones were still to be found here and there in the walls, and in one room a niche had been discovered which must formerly have held the statue of a saint.

The table was long and well polished. Daniel went down to the cellar to draw wine, brought glasses and filled them, and sat down in front of his brother.

"Your good health!"

"And yours."

Daniel always felt a little shy in front of Victor.

"You're going to tell me once again that I can't keep accounts and that I'm costing you a lot. . . ."

"You'll notice that I've said nothing to you yet."

"I'm going to Niort presently. I went there last week already. We've been using the same tractor for ten years now. It breaks down every two or three days. Sometimes I can mend it if I spend hours on the job. Other times I have to send for the mechanic.

"Last time I showed your wife my accounts she pointed out that this was becoming expensive. . . ."

"So you'd like to buy a new tractor."

"After ten years, I don't think that's too much to ask. I saw one at Niort that's a little more powerful and would be just the thing for the job."

"How much?"

"Fifteen thousand."

Victor Lecoin, rolling a cigarette, looked thoughtfully at his brother.

"How long will it take you to reduce it to the same state as the first?"

"Why not say right out that I'm incapable of driving a tractor? Anyhow, it's usually my wife who drives it."

For Véronique tackled every sort of job, plowing and mowing, with a red handkerchief tied around her head, and dressed, usually, in heavy blue jeans and a leather jacket.

"I'll do whatever you want, but I've warned you. Right now it's broken down and the self-starter and transmission need changing."

"Go and ask Jeanne for the money. I'll let her know."

"You're a good fellow, after all."

"After all?" queried Victor ironically.

"It's not easy to understand you. One never knows where one is with you, because one can't tell what you're thinking."

What was the good of telling Daniel that he was a failure and that without his brother's help he would probably be out of work?

"How is Father? I've just seen him in the kitchen garden, though it's still dark."

"He sticks to his habits."

Old Lecoin did not smoke or drink, but he always kept a bit of matchstick between his teeth.

"He doesn't grumble, and he eats well. Are you going to collect your mussels?"

"Yes."

"I gather you've got a new maid?"

"Since yesterday."

"I was told her boss got into trouble about her."

"Who told you that?"

"I don't remember. Somebody in the café, at Charron."

Daniel would willingly have spent all his time in cafés, not because he needed to drink—he was generally only a moderate drinker—but for the sake of the warm atmosphere, the buzz of voices, the smoke that quickly formed a haze overhead.

"When will the tractor be delivered?"

"Tomorrow. They can't manage it today because of the fair."

"When are you putting the cattle to pasture?"

"In about ten days. I'm waiting for the grass to grow a bit longer."

"And the sheep?"

These were in what was known as the lower meadow, by the seashore. There were about fifteen of them.

"I sheared them last week."

"By yourself?"

"With Véronique."

Jeanne, too, helped her husband, but in a stiff, impersonal way. She did her duty scrupulously, without grumbling and apparently without enjoyment.

Véronique, on the other hand, was good-humored and always merry, and when she looked at her husband it was plain that she was in love with him and was ready to forgive him for everything.

"Are any of your cows about to calve?"

"Two of them'll calve this month and another next month. I'll wait till they're out at pasture and then I'll sell three or four of the calves, otherwise we'll be short of space."

Victor had other properties, some of them several miles away, which he leased to butchers from La Rochelle to fatten their beasts there.

He had no faith in banks, still less in the bonds and securities that had ruined Charles de Rosy. He invested the money he earned in good land.

41

When there was nothing for sale in the neighborhood he bought gold pieces and stored them in bottles which, when they were full, he buried by night in places known only to himself and his wife.

He poured himself another glass and tossed it off.

"I'll go back and tell Jeanne. Don't let yourself be swindled. So long."

He walked out heavily and climbed into his car.

Jeanne was already in the office. Upstairs, Alice could be heard moving about as she did the bedroom.

"Daniel's coming to ask you for some money. Apparently the tractor's finished and he's going to buy a new one at Niort."

She uttered no protest.

"How much?"

"Fifteen thousand francs."

"I have enough in the safe."

It was an old, very large, very heavy safe, one of the kind that an even moderately skillful burglar could have opened in no time.

"Is Doudou here?"

"A moment ago he was washing the trucks."

He stood hesitating in the hallway, and finally decided to go up to the first floor and into his bedroom, where Alice was making the bed, bending over it.

"I forgot my handkerchief"; he felt it necessary to explain his presence, which was not in character for him.

He took one from the drawer of the chest. She looked

at him seriously, as if she were asking herself what she had to anticipate from him.

"Do you like the house?"

"It is practical."

"Do you know how to cook?"

"Only simple dishes, Madame teaches me, she is very nice with me."

"I'll try to be the same."

He left the room, somewhat ashamed of himself. If you came down to it, hadn't he just tried to court this brat? He would have preferred to put her out of his mind, but her image kept coming back to him. His wife, who had heard him go up the stairs, must have put two and two together, she guessed everything. This was what he disliked in her. He had hardly known his mother, who died shortly after Daniel's birth, when he himself was not yet six.

Little by little, Jeanne had ceased to be his wife, taking over more or less the role of the mother. A tolerant mother but lacking warmth and tenderness. He had never known tenderness, no one had given it to him; his father barely paid any attention to him. The old man could neither read nor write. He rarely went to the café, he spoke little, and only when it was necessary.

Was he of limited intelligence? It was possible, even probable. He lived a little like Doudou, though he slept in the house and took his meals at their table.

Lecoin sat down in the passage, beside the coatrack, to

pull on his high boots and then made his way to the garage, where the deaf-mute was wiping the windshield of the smaller truck and greeted him with a broad smile.

A dazzling sun made the sea sparkle; in the distance could be seen the sails of fishing boats dragging their nets.

The water had withdrawn a little farther than the previous day, uncovering the shingle, with pools of mud, and a thick layer of green seaweed clung to the base of the mussel-bed stakes.

There were a great many old women in the oyster beds, working as if they were doing their housework, tidying up, removing the larger stones. There were men, too, wearing hip boots like Lecoin's.

This was his favorite moment of the day. Doudou and he shared the work without any need of speech. In a couple of hours they filled seven hampers of mussels, which Doudou carried to the truck. The season was in full swing. From May onward business would cease almost entirely until the return of the months with an R in them.

He was not conscious of any thoughts. From his oyster bed he collected a basketful for lunch. He could eat five or six dozen by himself.

"How much are you giving for them today?"

"Two francs more per hamper than yesterday. How much have you got?"

"Eight hampers full."

He pulled his big wallet out of his pocket and counted the notes. Doudou had understood and came to get old Mathieu's hampers. People came up, one after the other, and argued over the price, but they could not resist the sight of that thick wallet.

He collected some thirty hampers in all and went off toward the village, stopping as usual in front of Mimile's. The card players were there. Lecoin raised a hand in greeting while the others mumbled: "Hi!"

Doudou went off to sit at the far end of the bar. It had become a rite. Théo Porchet was there again, but he avoided sniggering or making any unpleasant remarks.

Théo was a little over forty, and his companions were about the same age. They were all from Marsilly and they had been playmates and classmates at school.

This was the case, too, with those who played cards in the afternoon. These were the old fellows, the over-seventies who had known one another from childhood. After so many years they still gathered around the same tavern table to play auction *manille,* and there were always two or three more sitting astride their rush-seated chairs watching and commenting on the game.

This went on year in, year out.

The morning sessions included, among others, Jo Chevalier, the barber, who was also verger at the church. Then there was Louis Cardis, who owned a small farm, four or five head of cattle, chiefly looked after by his wife.

As for little Marcel Lefranc, he was a pork butcher

and traveled around the farms killing pigs and, if required to, cooking them.

Pringuet, the postman, only looked on for a few minutes before resuming his round.

Lecoin found his glass ready filled in front of him; he sipped it while he watched them. Through the glazed door he could see Mimile's wife in her checked apron polishing her brass. One day was set aside for this each week, as for everything else, Monday being reserved for washing not only at Mimile's but in every house in the village and at all the neighboring farms.

Then you could see the walls surrounded by long rows of white linen bellying out in the wind.

Why did he think of this? Perhaps indirectly because he was thinking about Alice. Would she do the washing, like their former maid, or was she not strong enough for that?

He finished his wine and wiped his mouth. Then he moved toward the door, muttering in his turn:

"So long. So long, Mimile!"

And of course Doudou followed him, barefooted, silent.

He drove straight to Charron, passing his house without stopping. He saw nobody through the open windows. His wife's office looked out on the courtyard. Alice must have been in the kitchen.

At Charron there were five or six trucks on the beach. He went right up to the mussel beds, waiting for the men to speak to him.

"Same price as yesterday?"

"Two francs more per hamper."

"I've got ten."

The deaf-mute read the words on people's lips and never misunderstood. Nobody had taught him anything. He had grown like a wild plant and that was probably why he chose to live by himself in his hut.

They collected another fifteen hampers, and by noon the two men were home again. While Doudou set to work washing the mussels Lecoin took the hamper of oysters into the kitchen.

"You can serve these at lunch."

She first said, meekly: "All right." Then she ventured:

"There's casserole of veal all ready."

"Well, we'll start with the oysters."

She was staring at them in embarrassment, and he guessed.

"Have you never opened oysters?"

"No."

"I'll show you."

There was an oyster knife in the drawer. He used it skillfully, leaving no beard behind.

"Did you see?"

"Yes. I'm afraid."

"Of what?"

"Of cutting myself."

"Try in front of me."

She held the knife awkwardly, and he took her hand and placed it on the handle.

"Now slip the blade in here."

She did not succeed right away, but after about a dozen attempts she had got the knack and looked up gratefully at her master.

This was the first sign he had had from her, for the previous day she had scarcely looked at him. What did she think of him? That he was like Paquot, like all men, and that someday he was going to demand what he considered his right?

He was determined to avoid that. And in any case she was too young and too thin for him. He went into the office.

"I brought some oysters for lunch."

"We've already got . . ."

"I know: casserole of veal."

"Who's going to open them?"

This was a task she had never succeeded in performing, for she had a horror of knives.

"Alice."

"D'you think she'll know how to?"

"I've shown her. She'll manage."

"Do you need the car this afternoon?"

"No. I'm taking a truckload of mussels to the station."

"Take the key, in case you get home before us. I'm going to take Alice in to town to buy her some underwear and a few clothes. She's got practically nothing but what she stands up in."

"D'you think she's going to do?"

"She's very willing. Once she has got used to the house . . ."

They lunched rather later than usual because of the time it took to open so many oysters. Lecoin ate six dozen, which did not prevent him from doing honor to the braised veal.

His wife went upstairs presently to dress, while he rolled a cigarette and drank the coffee that Alice brought him. He watched her coming and going between the kitchen and the dining room, and his glance always ended by dwelling on her long, thin, bare legs. There was a bruise on her left shin. She must have given herself a knock, somehow.

He would have liked to chat with her, but she had to be tamed first, particularly after her experience at Surgères.

"Have you had some oysters?"

"No. I've never tasted any."

"Are there some left in the kitchen?"

"Yes."

"Try some."

"They've got such a funny texture."

"You'll get used to that. Come here. I'll show you how to get them out of the shell."

He showed her, and held out an oyster ready to eat. She hesitated, looked at him with some embarrassment, and eventually swallowed the oyster.

"Well?"

"It's not bad."

"Eat as many as you like. They'll make you strong."

He smiled at her. It was unusual to see him smile. When he was on a spree, as last night, he sometimes laughed, but it was too loud and forced a laugh. He had to pretend to be enjoying himself. Perhaps, indeed, he was trying to make himself believe it.

Jeanne came down, wearing a black dress, with her black coat over her arm.

"Hurry, Alice, will you? We're going to town together."

She stopped eating the oysters, and Jeanne looked at her husband as though she guessed the scene that had just taken place. She was not annoyed about it. The embarrassing thing was that she always knew everything.

"Have you got to go anywhere?" she asked.

"Only to the station."

The pendulum clock in the living room was striking two, and Lecoin made his way to the garage, where the deaf-mute was finishing washing the mussels. No one ever knew when he ate. He was always available, and he did not like anyone to go into his hut.

When all the hampers were loaded and labeled he climbed into his place in the front of the truck and Lecoin started the motor. They drove through Nieul and passed the school where Jeanne had been a teacher. How long ago it seemed! How many boys and girls had been there since, who were now fathers and mothers of families!

50

He went to collect his certificates, as he had done the previous day, and then helped Doudou carry the hampers to the weighing machine.

At the cash desk, once again, he pulled out his old wallet. It was barely four o'clock. The tide was nearly high and the biggest boats would soon be coming into harbor, while the little ones, which drew less water, still went on fishing.

He had not forgotten his key, and he went into the house to take off his boots and put on a pair of shoes. After this he returned to the garage and took out the second truck. The day before, he had heard a noise that puzzled him, and raising the hood, he began to examine the motor.

To begin with, he tightened the transmission belt. As the noise still went on, he took out the carburetor and set about adjusting it.

He liked tinkering with things. In fact, he liked doing all sorts of things, except playing cards, for instance, or sitting in a café. He nearly always chose a bar where he could stand up at the counter.

When the carburetor was back in place he went to try out the truck on the road, and drove on as far as Marans, a little town he liked, among fields, on the edge of an unused canal.

He stopped close to the bridge and went for a drink at the corner bistrot, where he was well known. The proprietor was in shirt sleeves, like Mimile, but older and stouter than he was, with white hair that emphasized the redness of his face.

He liked to drink with his customers, so that toward five in the afternoon his speech tended to become slurred.

Here, too, there were card players, local characters who scarcely spoke as they played.

"Is it true you've taken on the girl from Paquot's?"

He disliked that sort of question and answered with a brief nod.

"Aren't you afraid?"

He shrugged his shoulders and made no reply. So the news had spread throughout the district. It was not he who had chosen Alice, but his wife. Was it necessary for him to tell them that? And to add that he had no intention of laying a finger on her?

"Lucky break for Paquot. He might have got a prison sentence if the magistrate hadn't been such a decent fellow. . . ."

Children were playing in the street with shrill cries, just as in the school yard at recess. It was a bright, mild spring day. A young woman went past, going to pay a call no doubt, for she was in her Sunday best, wearing white cotton gloves.

He emptied his glass and went back to his truck.

"Get moving, you old fool."

He could not have said whether he was addressing the truck or himself in these terms. There were days when he felt out of spirits, and when he thought about things too much he had the blues.

What was missing in his life? He had started from nothing, from less than nothing. At thirteen he worked on a farm where he looked after the horses, for tractors were still uncommon, indeed almost unknown, in the region.

There were two other farm hands, and they all three slept in the loft, where each of them had his iron bed. It was rather like his later experience of barracks life. The two men were coarse-spoken and the stories they told one another, ignoring his presence, still made him blush.

It was here that he had seen sex for the first time, between one of these laborers and a farm girl who had been taken on recently and who slept in a neighboring attic.

"Now d'you see how to go about it, kid?"

This man was still alive. Victor had seen him one day when he was passing through Lhoumaux, weaving unsteadily across the road.

Lecoin had worked hard, harder than anyone else he knew. He had endured a great deal, too.

When he was a tenant farmer at Four Winds, he had done all the work with his wife to avoid having to pay a farm hand, and Jeanne had done her share of the plowing.

It was odd that they hadn't become closer friends. Not that there was any hostility between them. They lived side by side without quarreling or criticizing one another, but apart from their work there seemed to be no bond between them.

In the evening they usually settled down in front of the

television set, and they might spend two hours watching a program without exchanging a word.

On the way home he stopped at Four Winds Farm. His father was cleaning out the stable, while Véronique was busy in the kitchen.

"Isn't Daniel back?"

"Anyone would think you didn't know him. When he goes to the fair . . ."

"I know. I hope he's chosen his tractor wisely."

"It's an American machine. They're supposed to be the strongest. The old one was always breaking down. What'll you have to drink? A brandy?"

"No. A drop of wine, since you ask me. What are you making?"

"Pastry for a *quiche lorraine.*"

She was fresh and blooming, with a frank, direct smile, and looked younger than her thirty-eight years. Did his brother deserve such a wife? Wouldn't he, Victor, have been worthier of her?

He had never made advances to her, of course, but he enjoyed looking at her while he sipped his wine.

"How's Father?"

"Didn't you see him?"

"Yes, but I didn't ask him, because I'd just have been snapped at."

"He's quite well. He works a bit slower than he used to, maybe, but he can still do a good day's work."

"Still as much of a chatterbox?"

"You could count the words he utters in twenty-four hours."

"Does he still smarten himself up on Sunday to go for his drink at the café?"

"Sure. He sits down by himself in a corner and orders his half-liter. He doesn't join any group. He stays there with his back to the wall, staring around him and trying to disentangle the buzz of talk. He comes back punctually for dinner and before coming to table he goes off to change. By the way, how are you getting on with your new maid?"

"Jeanne has taken her in to town to buy her some clothes and underwear."

"Is she pretty?"

"No."

"That's bad luck for you."

He had a reputation for running after the girls, and it was true that he had done so ever since he was fifteen. In the past thirty years he'd had sex, even if only on a single furtive occasion, with half the women in Marsilly.

It was something he could not help. He wanted every woman he saw, perhaps because it reassured him. But about what did it reassure him? What could he still have to worry about?

As he had heard one peasant woman tell another, he was "the rich man" of the village and he went on buying land when there was any for sale, or sealing up gold coins in bottles.

He was not miserly, but he had known poverty too well not to be afraid of it, so that he forearmed himself against it.

Jeanne had understood this, and that was probably why she helped him to the best of her ability. And when he went out at night to bury another bottle, it was she who held the flashlight.

He might have stopped working and lived on his income, on the rent from his farm and his lands.

And then? What would he have done all day long? Played cards at Mimile's for hours, drinking one glass after another?

He was like his father, who had rejected his offer of an allowance, saying with a shake of the head:

"I've always worked and I shall go on working until death takes me."

They tried in vain to spare the old man the heavy work. He was, as it were, challenging himself.

There was a slight mystery concerning him. His married life had lasted only six years. At thirty, soon after Daniel's birth, he had been left a widower.

But as far back as Victor's memory would reach he could not recall his father having any love affairs. News spread fast in the village. If he had had a mistress the whole neighborhood would have known about it.

Was it out of loyalty to his wife's memory? This was possible, and indeed Victor thought it likely. He had only seen a single photograph of his mother in the old man's room, the one that had been taken on their wedding day, for at that time few people owned cameras, and photographs were taken only on special occasions.

Under her white veil, she was wearing a long dress with puffed sleeves, and her expression was tinged with melancholy. Was this an attempt to look distinguished? Or was she already suffering from her fatal complaint, unknown to herself or her husband?

Victor was not even sure what she had died of. At the time he had been told no details, for he was too young. Later on, he would not have dared question his father on the subject. Even today, he would not have the courage to do so.

When he got home the Peugeot was already back in the garage. He went into the office, where he found his wife; she had changed her dress.

"That didn't take long."

"I didn't buy her a whole outfit but just the essentials. It wasn't easy. She's so thin that they sent me to the schoolgirls' department."

"Did she talk to you?"

"No more than was absolutely necessary. Perhaps it'll be different when we've won her confidence, if we ever do win it."

When he met Alice a little later she was wearing a checked apron like his sister-in-law Véronique, which came halfway down her legs and thus changed her completely. She had suddenly become less of a child and more of a young woman.

"What are we having?"

"Pea soup and a cheese omelette."

"Will you be able to make that?"

"Madame will show me."

She neither smiled nor sulked. Her attitude was irreproachable.

CHAPTER 3

It was Sunday, but Lecoin got up as early as usual, although he had nothing to do. Jeanne was downstairs already, and a delicious smell of coffee floated up.

He could have sworn that on Sundays the air felt different and the sky seemed emptier. There was no sound to be heard except the occasional crowing of a cock close by or in the distance.

He dawdled over his dressing on Sundays, and instead of a quick shower he liked to linger in a warm bath. Instead of his usual clothes he put on a white shirt and a black suit, which was beginning to feel a little tight.

When he came down his wife was not yet dressed, and

this again was part of the ritual. His place was set. He drank his cup of coffee first, looking around in search of Alice and listening to the sounds that came from the kitchen.

It was she who brought him his soup, and then his bacon and eggs. She was wearing one of the checked aprons that had been bought the day before.

Was it only an impression? It seemed to him that she dared not look him in the face. Did she think all men were like Paquot? Or was it just that she needed time to settle down?

Jeanne, sitting opposite him, had already eaten. She said:

"She's asked me if she might go to Mass. I said yes, of course."

"Which Mass?"

"The nine o'clock one."

This was the second Mass. There was another, a low Mass, at seven. The Lecoins were not churchgoers. Jeanne had gone for a few months in the early days of their marriage, then she had stopped going, but they were none the less on good terms with the curé.

It was Victor who went to feed the hens and collect the eggs. As always on a Sunday, he felt at loose ends. He missed his customary activities and did not know what to do with his great hulk of a body.

When he went back into the house Jeanne had gone up to dress. So had Alice, no doubt, for she was nowhere to be seen, and when she came down again she was wearing a navy blue dress brightened by a little round collar of white rep.

It had changed her. He could not recognize the little slattern he had met the first day, and he was sorry, though he could scarcely have said why. Her hair was tidily dressed and her skin seemed clearer.

A little later he caught sight of Doudou in the courtyard. He, too, was wearing a dark suit, a shirt, and a tie. It was the only day in the week when Doudou did not go barefoot, and it had not been easy to find shoes for him, for he took the largest size.

Nobody knew exactly how he spent his Sundays. Sometimes he was to be seen waiting for the bus to La Rochelle. What could he find to do there when the streets were almost empty, except at churchtime, and all the shops were shut? At other times he would stay in the neighborhood, always by himself, ending up, like Lecoin's father, sitting on a chair at Mimile's and watching the card players.

Where did he eat? Whom did he meet? This was a minor mystery that Victor had never solved.

On weekdays he followed his master like a great faithful dog, but he kept his Sundays for himself and did not reappear until the evening.

Lecoin was not unhappy. He loved life, breathing it in through every pore. Yet the emptiness of Sundays always depressed him somewhat, and now there was this Alice business in the bargain.

He had to restrain himself forcibly from constantly

going into the kitchen. He needed to feel her presence, to see her, to know that she was within reach.

She went up to help Jeanne do the bedroom and bathroom, and when she had finished it was time to go to church. Jeanne had even bought her, the day before, a funny little white hat which she wore awkwardly, as if she had never had a hat before.

Through the window he watched her going off. Then Jeanne came down, dressed in black. She, too, was different. She looked like a worthy middle-aged bourgeoise who had put on weight, and her face was slightly made up. A faint scent of lavender hung about her.

"What shall we do? I've got nothing in for lunch."

It was almost a tradition. On Sunday mornings they took the car, like so many other people, and went off along highways and byways.

Sometimes they drove toward the Vendée, through the marshes, and had lunch at Luçon or Fontenay-le-Comte, or even at Les Sables d'Olonne. Other times they went toward the south. They drove slowly, hardly speaking, staring vaguely at the familiar landscape that flowed past them.

"We might go and have some chowder."

This was the specialty of Fouras, a few miles from La Rochelle. It was a kind of bouillabaisse with a basis of small soles, eels, and cuttlefish.

"We'll decide on the way."

He got the car out and she took her seat by his side. She looked imposing thus, with her regular, somewhat stern features, and she sat very straight, looking as dignified as if she were in the back of a chauffeur-driven limousine.

They drove all around La Rochelle, through the arcaded streets that they knew so well, for the mere pleasure of being on the move, of seeing dark-clad people making their way to various churches or queuing up at the only patisserie that was open.

All the boats were in harbor, and the fishermen, who were also at a loose end, hung about in little groups.

They crossed the railway bridge and went on driving toward Fouras. They got there far too early for lunch and drove on toward Rochefort.

The town was even quieter than La Rochelle.

"Shall we stop for a drink?"

"If you like."

They drew up on the main square and went into a corner café that they often visited.

He knew what his wife was going to have. It happened only once a week.

"One port and one half-liter of white wine," he ordered.

Here, too, there were card players. You found them everywhere, some joking and teasing one another, others taking the game very seriously.

And two couples, people like themselves, one with a small boy of five or six who had demanded a straw through which he was drinking a grenadine, like Doudou.

The weather was still fine, the sky an almost cloudless blue with only a slight, almost luminous mist on the horizon.

"I think she'll do. She's very willing. I feel that before this she's been terrorized."

"Has she just had the one place?"

"Yes; when she went to Surgères she'd just left the orphanage."

"Has she no relatives?"

"Apparently not. One fine morning her father and mother went off, leaving her in the packing case that was used for a cradle. It was in a shantytown somewhere outside Paris."

He would have liked to talk more about her, but now his wife fell silent, while he kept seeing, in his mind's eye, the slattern who had made so deep an impression on him that first day.

The proprietor, Léon, came to shake hands with them. He was a small, tubby fellow, very sure of himself, who had driven a taxi in Paris for many years and had finally come home to buy himself the café of his dreams.

"How're you keeping?"

"Very well, as usual."

"I keep going myself, except that my legs are beginning to swell. Seems that's due to standing up all day. Now, let's fill up your glasses. This one's on me."

"Not for me," Jeanne tried to protest.

"Nonsense! A drop of port never hurt anyone."

They were soon on their way back to Fouras, where

they always went to the same restaurant. This town was even emptier than the others. It was a summer resort with a long beach lined with little villas and boardinghouses.

There was no one on the beach except a couple of elderly peasants who had tucked up their trousers and were walking in the water. Perhaps it was the first time they had seen the sea. There were others like them in country districts, who never went farther than the nearest town, usually on a Saturday to do their shopping.

Lecoin's father, for instance, had never been farther afield than La Rochelle, except during his military service. Even taking the bus was quite an adventure for him. He was happy in his corner, and he stayed there. He needed nobody. He never seemed bored, and sometimes you could see his lips moving; he talked to himself.

They ate in the glass-fronted section of the restaurant, and after their fish chowder Victor had roast suckling pig, while his wife merely took a salad. She was a light eater and yet she was sturdily built. This was the more noticeable when she wore her Sunday best, a tightly fitting black dress.

An hour later they were back at La Rochelle, and they looked at the movie posters. They sometimes went to a movie, but none of those advertised seemed attractive to them.

"What shall we do?"

"Whatever you say."

They set off again, driving for the sake of the drive, and found themselves back at Fontenay-le-Comte. Were there people behind the closed doors and windows of those houses? It was like being in another world, where only the occasional car drove past. Close to the bridge, however, there was one man fishing, while two others watched him, leaning over the parapet.

"Shall we go home?"

He asked nothing better. He wanted to be near Alice again, to see her, to speak to her if possible, merely to say a few passing words to her so as to make contact. All day he had been missing her, and he felt sure Jeanne was aware of this.

Usually it did not embarrass him to have her guess his thoughts. On the contrary, it reassured him. It confirmed his sense that even when he went with prostitutes he was doing no harm, he was merely availing himself of his rights.

He was a normal man, for heaven's sake, perhaps somewhat more vigorous than most others. He was not troubled with prejudices. His life was his own business, and if anyone was to have the privilege of commenting on it it was Jeanne.

Now Jeanne had understood him long ago and she did not feel the need to weep or put on an air of resignation. Their association ran smoothly enough. He was fond of her. He respected her.

It was Jeanne who kept the key, and she took it from her handbag, since the front door was locked.

"She must have gone in through the kitchen."

But Alice was not in any of the ground-floor rooms, and the kitchen door was shut too.

The same thought struck them both. She had taken advantage of their absence to go off, God knows where. Probably the house had seemed too quiet for her, the daily routine boring.

He announced:

"I'm going to see if she's in her room."

Jeanne let him go up without comment. He went upstairs to the attic floor and knocked at the door of the maid's room. He got no answer and went in; he found the room tidy, with the checked apron laid out on the bed. There was an unfamiliar odor about the room, one that was new to the house—Alice's personal odor. In the wardrobe he found the black dress and another cotton dress that Jeanne must have bought her.

He heaved a sigh. He had been frightened. If she had decided to leave for good she would have taken her personal possessions with her.

"She's not there," he said when he came down again. "She hasn't taken her things. She must have gone for a walk."

"What shall we do? Shall we watch television?"

The set had been acquired only recently, and it stood in the living room, where they never sat except to watch a program.

"I'm going to walk down to the sea first."

He often did so. He would walk past Mimile's and go

on as far as the shingle beach, where the stakes of the mussel beds were not yet submerged.

In the far distance a figure was outlined; it was a woman, walking slowly over the shingle and from time to time flinging a stone into the sea.

He thought he recognized Alice's figure. He dared not go to meet her, nor did he dare wait for her so that they could go through the village and return home together.

He set off again, but this time he opened the door of the bistrot and went in. There was a far greater crowd than on weekdays and a buzz of voices as if everyone was talking at once.

The *belote* players were in their usual place and, opposite them, the old guard playing *manille*. And there were others who were only to be seen on Sundays.

He went to lean back against the counter. The air was blue with smoke, and Mimile had to keep climbing down through the trap door to fill bottles from the cask.

Everyone looked at Victor, greeting him or waving to him. There was in the villagers' attitude a kind of respect which might be due either to his strength or to his wealth.

This did not mean that they liked him. If tomorrow he should lose his money or fall ill, surely most of them would be delighted?

He emptied his glass and refilled it. He glanced at the tables one after the other, and meanwhile kept watch on the road.

In a few minutes she would pass in front of Mimile's on her way home. She had gone for a walk all alone, along the beach. What could she have been thinking about? And what sort of future did she envisage?

She had happened on a quiet, respectable house where she was not ill-treated or overworked. Was she happy? Was she still a bit frightened of him, because of what had happened at Surgères?

He would have liked to think about something else. He tried to follow one of the games of cards but could not take an interest in it.

She walked slowly past the café, and others besides himself stared at her. Instinctively, he glanced at Théo, who winked at him insolently, as if to say: "So the kid's got spruced up a bit!"

Théo was the same age as himself. They had gone to school together and had always detested one another, although probably neither could have said why.

On Théo's side it must have been due to envy, for he had been a puny child, at the bottom of the class. His father had kept the hardware store and his mother was a stout woman who had ended her days as an invalid, in an armchair at the back of the shop.

"Fill it up, Mimile."

He had no wish to get drunk, but it would take more than a few half-liters a day to make him lose his self-control.

It simply put a different color on his thoughts. The world became gentler, and he began thinking about Alice not lustfully but with a kind of tenderness.

He might have had a daughter of her age, or even a

married daughter with children. Was that what he had missed?

A train of such disconnected images passed through his mind.

He watched all these men sitting or standing around him and wondered if there were any real friends among them. They clapped one another on the shoulder when they met, they called one another *tu* and used Christian names, they recalled memories of their boyhood and youth.

"D'you remember Lavaud and the way he died?"

Lavaud had been hit by a truck while he was drunk. He had died in the ambulance that was taking him to La Rochelle.

Lecoin finished his drink and drew his old wallet from his pocket. He noticed one of his neighbors nudging another.

He was "the rich man," as that old woman had said. And what then? Had he taken anything away from anyone? He was hard to please, perhaps, about the quality of the mussels he bought, but he paid more for them than others did and he had to cope with the washing and shipping of them.

Four Winds Farm had brought in more when he worked it himself, and he'd have found it more profitable to choose a different tenant.

What would have become of his brother? It was for the sake of Daniel and his wife and of their father that he had forgone the greater profit.

That reminded him that he had not yet seen the new tractor. He drove past his own house and on to Four Winds Farm. He found Véronique alone.

"Daniel out?"

"As usual on Sundays," she sighed with a resigned smile.

"Have they brought the tractor?"

"Last night. Would you like to see it?"

"Is Father out too?"

"He'll be back soon, to look after the cows. He must be at the bistrot at Esnandes."

He went to look at the tractor in the shed. It was a fine powerful machine, painted red.

"He's made a good choice, hasn't he?"

"He's chosen the most expensive thing there was."

"But the strongest, too. I'm longing to drive it. I'm like a small boy who's just been bought a new bicycle."

"You'll soon have the chance."

For she was in charge of both plowing and harvesting. It was not as it had been in his youth, when three or four farm hands were needed and at harvest time all the farmers of the village came over to help, as well as the threshers.

He sometimes regretted the days when he ran the farm himself. He resented his brother's lack of interest in it.

"Have you had lunch at home?" he asked his sister-in-law.

"Yes, all by myself, because he hasn't been back since

this morning. Heaven knows what state he'll be in when he gets home."

She bore him no ill will. Life was like that.

"How's Jeanne?"

"Very well."

"And the new maid?"

"She seems to be getting used to us. She doesn't talk much, but that may be just shyness."

"It's a bit of luck for her, being with you."

She said this without irony.

"Will you have a drink?"

"No, thanks. I've just had a half-liter at Mimile's."

When he got home Alice was in the kitchen, wearing her checked apron, busily peeling potatoes. He could not see Jeanne, who must have been in the living room watching television.

"Have you had a good Sunday?"

"Oh, yes!"

For the first time, she showed some sign of satisfaction.

"What did you do after Mass?"

"I came back and got myself something to eat."

"Didn't you find it strange being all alone in the house?"

"No. After that I slept a little, then I went for a walk along the beach. I'd hardly seen the sea before. There was nobody else there. I had the whole shore to myself."

Why was he so disturbed? Why did he not dare linger any longer in the kitchen?

"What's for supper?"

"Mutton with potatoes and cabbage."

"D'you know how to cook it?"

"Yes."

He joined Jeanne in the living room and drew up a chair beside her. An American movie was being shown; he had missed the first half and didn't understand it at all.

A week later, the situation had not changed. The neap tide had come and the sea was so still that there was hardly anything to be done in the mussel beds. For five whole days he had not carried any hampers in to La Rochelle.

He was not idle, however. There was work to be done in the kitchen garden, which was huge, while Doudou painted the sliding doors of the garage light green.

He was obsessed by the thought of Alice. This disconcerted him, for it had never happened to him in his life before. He had had a great many women, of every sort, including hers, but none of them had disturbed his equilibrium in the least.

He had never uttered the word "love," and in any case he did not believe in that.

From early morning, he felt compelled to go into the kitchen on some pretext or other, for he had reached the point of seeking pretexts for his actions.

And it was not so much on account of Jeanne, who pretended to notice nothing, as for the sake of Alice herself.

When she was wearing her checked apron, as she did every day now, he kept thinking of the black dress and that business with Paquot.

The scene had become so imprinted on his mind that the least thing set him off, and then he dared not look anyone in the face.

Did the girl realize this? He could not tell. She did her work conscientiously but in silence, and when she did speak it was only to answer a question as briefly as possible.

"Did you sleep well?"

"Yes."

"Your room's not too cold?"

"I've never slept in a heated room."

In the middle of the morning, when she was doing the bedroom, he would find some excuse for going up, like any schoolboy. It mortified him. He would say nothing to her. Or else: "I've forgotten my handkerchief."

She moved around the bed to pull the sheets straight and bent forward, showing her thin legs.

Was she aware of what was happening? If she was, she displayed neither pride nor satisfaction nor annoyance. In fact her face expressed nothing at all.

He was convinced that his wife knew, for nothing escaped her, and he found this humiliating. He would almost rather she had protested.

He continued to drop in at Mimile's toward eleven o'clock, and the deaf-mute accompanied him automatically, always barefoot although there were a couple of days of cold rain.

Lecoin might have been mistaken, but he had got it into his head that if Théo looked at him with an increasingly sarcastic air it was because he was watching the progress of his disease.

For it really was a disease. He resented it. He was ashamed of himself for acting in so deceitful, secretive a way.

During the neap tides Jeanne, too, had less work to do in the office, and she took advantage of this to work in the house. Among other things she washed all the net curtains, which she then had to iron and hang again.

All this was part of the usual springtime tasks.

On Wednesday, in a fit of fury against himself, he had gone off to La Rochelle in the late afternoon, announcing:

"Don't expect me back for dinner."

She knew what that meant and she should have been surprised, for it generally happened only at the end of the week.

He went to Nénette's.

"Hello, you here already!"

Nénette was the one to show surprise.

"You know, dearie, I haven't got much to offer you. A brandy in the meanwhile?"

There was a girl at the bar whom he did not know, a small brunette who seemed to be waiting for someone.

"Let me make one or two phone calls."

She went into the other room and he overheard scraps of what she was saying.

"Since I'm telling you it's worth your while . . . No, no! . . . You'll see. . . . No, you don't know him. . . . Well, are you coming right away?"

She served him a second glass and, with a glance, indicated the girl sitting at the bar.

"She's all right. She doesn't usually do it. And the one who's coming is a piece I'd like your views on."

He felt like shrugging his shoulders. One or the other, what did he care? All he wanted was to stop thinking about Alice and, as he promised himself, to get blind drunk.

"Got any champagne keeping cool?

"Always, dearie. If anyone nice turns up while you're upstairs I'll send her up."

"It's not worth it."

This, too, infuriated him. What did Jeanne think of this escapade? Did she understand why he needed it? And in that case, wasn't she a bit frightened?

Provided she didn't think it a wise precaution to get rid of Alice during his absence! This was the first solution that occurred to him, the only one, in fact, and all because of that swine Paquot.

He had to wait for the girl nearly half an hour, watching the umbrellas file past along the quayside. She was, in fact, quite unlike a professional. She might have been

76

between twenty and twenty-two, and she was very fresh-looking, with a shy smile.

"Mlle Fernande . . . M. Victor . . ."

She held out a gloved hand and then seemed to wait for what would happen next.

"Suppose you go into the back room, my dears? It's more comfortable, and I'll bring you the champagne."

As they were moving toward the little parlor the girl who was sitting at the bar realized, with surprise, that she was invited to join them. At this Fernande frowned, and made as though to leave the place.

"No, no, love. You'll see that you'll all three have a good time."

She had blushed. It took several glasses of champagne to loosen her tongue.

Finally they went upstairs. Fernande went into the bathroom to undress, while the other girl took off her clothes without embarrassment.

Both of them had good figures. Nénette brought up two bottles of champagne, to which Lecoin did more honor than the others.

He took Fernande first, and he did so angrily, almost savagely. She looked at him in some anxiety, and the other girl, too, was surprised. He wanted to take his revenge.

Revenge for what? For the fix into which he had got himself. For having been reduced to cheating like a naughty boy in order to enjoy forbidden things.

He stayed upstairs longer than the previous week and drank a whole bottle by himself.

"Why are you so on edge?"

"Who says I'm on edge?"

"It's obvious, surely? Have you quarreled with your wife?"

"My wife and I never quarrel."

"Does she know you're here?"

"Yes."

"And she doesn't mind?"

"No."

"Is she ugly?"

"No."

"Have you been married a long time?"

"Over twenty years."

"When did you begin deceiving her?"

"I don't deceive her."

His nerves were raw. After a couple of hours he had had enough of the two women, and went to take out his wallet from his jacket pocket. He was more generous than usual, as though to make up for having been ungracious.

"You can get dressed again, girls."

As for him, he sat down in a velvet-covered armchair by the window and rolled himself a cigarette. Night had fallen, and the rain distorted the beams of light outside.

"Aren't you coming down?"

"Not yet."

"Shall we see you again?"

"Surely."

He had not switched on the light. The room was lit only by the street lamps outside. He smoked his cigarette slowly, with a gloomy look, and only stood up at last to make sure that there was nothing left in the bottles. They were empty, including the third that Nénette had brought up.

He went down the winding staircase and he almost fell, for he was not walking quite steadily.

"A brandy!" he ordered.

When he turned around he saw the girl who had been at the bar sitting in the little parlor with a man. As for Fernande, she had disappeared.

"Well, what did I tell you, dearie? That was something worth while, eh?"

He shrugged his shoulders.

"Look here, you're getting very choosy."

"I'm fed up."

"With what?"

"With everything."

"That's not like my old pal Victor. You're usually in better spirits than this. Something bothering you?"

"No."

"It's not your wife?"

"No."

"You're big and strong and you're rich, what more do you want?"

He could not explain to her that all he wanted was a little slut of a girl who'd let herself be fondled by a swine like Paquot, and who had not protested when he had put his tool in her hand.

He promised himself never to do that. He vowed he would never touch her, but he was aware of the fragile nature of his resolution.

"Another brandy."

"Are you sure?"

"Am I tight?"

"Not yet, but not far off. I only mention it because you've got to drive."

"Pour me one all the same. I'm used to it, after all these years."

"Knowing you as I do, and seeing you in this state, you'll be back to see me before long."

It was true, but he did not like being told so. It irritated him to find people trying to guess his thoughts, explain his actions.

"What do I owe you?"

She had made out his bill on a sheet from a writing pad.

"So long," he muttered as he left the bar.

"No hard feelings?"

He seemed to hesitate, and finally sighed: "Not toward you."

There were moments when his resentment was directed against Alice. He did not even know how his wife had come to engage her. He dared not ask, for it would have betrayed his excessive interest in the girl.

He felt hungry. He went into a small café behind the

Big Clock tower and had a couple of ham sandwiches with a glass of beer. Here again, people were playing cards, and it began to annoy him. There they were, smugly looking at their hands, making their bids with an air of triumph, laying down each card as if such a gesture were of major importance.

Such people must feel at peace with the world. And there were others like them everywhere. They never felt lost, as he did at that moment. Did they even have a home life? Their home was the corner table, always in the same café and with the same partners.

He paid and went out, sick at heart. He hesitated for a moment, not immediately remembering where he had left his car. He had taken the Peugeot, and out of habit he was looking for the truck.

Instead of sobering him up, the fresh air increased his tipsiness, and he nearly flooded the engine when he started it up. Fortunately, he was soon out of the town and he met only two other cars on the way home.

He drove the Peugeot into the garage and turned up the collar of his jacket, for it was raining harder than ever. He went into the warm house, and then, after shaking himself dry, went into the dining room. The table was still set, for one person. Jeanne had had her meal.

Alice stood in the doorway.

"What would you like me to bring you? Madame had eggs and some cheese."

"I've had dinner in town." He added, hesitantly: "Thank you, Alice."

Music sounded vaguely in the background. It came from the living room. He went across the hallway and found his wife in front of the television set.

"You're back?"

"As you see. I haven't been reported missing."

It was idiotic. Merely from this remark and the tone in which he said it, Jeanne could clearly see that he was drunk.

"Have you had anything to eat?"

"Two big ham sandwiches."

"Shall we go upstairs? In any case the program isn't interesting. I was watching it to pass the time while I waited for you."

"I feel like sleep, anyhow."

"So do I."

"You're a good woman, Jeanne."

She did not answer. She knew what that sentimental tone implied.

"If you weren't so young I'd say you're a mother to me. I never knew my mother, you see, and if she were to come back to life I shouldn't be able to recognize her."

"Come along."

"Wait till I've said good night to Alice. She's a good little thing. It was bad luck she should happen on a swine like Paquot."

"Alice has gone up to bed."

"Five minutes ago she asked me what I wanted to eat."

"Go and look in the kitchen."

Jeanne was right. The lights were out, and the young girl's footsteps sounded on the staircase.

He stumbled over the first step and had to save himself with his hands. Even though Jeanne pretended not to have noticed, he felt mortified.

He was drunker than usual and he undressed clumsily, letting his clothes drop to the floor and leaving them there. His wife picked them up without a word and hung them up.

"Won't you take some bicarbonate of soda?"

"No."

He sometimes suffered from heartburn when he had drunk too much, and she dosed him with bicarbonate.

"It's quite true what I was saying to you downstairs. You'd have made a wonderful mother."

"Go to sleep now."

He fell asleep so quickly that he did not hear Jeanne undress. Next day, for once, he had a slight hangover and felt less than ever at peace with himself.

The week dragged on thus. In the morning he would go and have a look at the mussel beds. The wind had turned. The sea was heavier. There was a long fringe of seaweed on the shingle, marking the limits of the tide.

Then he would work in the garden. The soil was heavy. There was a whole patch at the end that needed clearing. At Daniel's place this job was done by his father, who would spend hours bending over the flower beds.

What happiness had the old man had? What happiness did he still get from life? He had doubtless been in love with his wife, but she had died after only a few years. Since then, he was not known to have had any love affairs. He worked from sunrise to sunset, and his only diversion was going on a Sunday to sit in a corner at the Esnandes bistrot.

Lecoin felt rebellious, without knowing exactly why. He went to the house to pour himself a glass of wine. The two women were in the kitchen, facing one another over the ironing. He noticed that Alice happened to be ironing one of his shirts, and this had a peculiar effect on him, as though it had set up a certain intimacy between them.

He went back to work in the kitchen garden. The deaf-mute was now painting the inside of the garage doors, and toward half past eleven Lecoin only had to show himself to be understood.

They were going off together to Mimile's, one to drink a half-liter of wine, the other his lemonade with grenadine.

Around the card tables he saw only three men, who seemed to be waiting for something.

"Isn't Cardis here?" he asked in surprise.

"He broke his leg, falling off his tractor. We're waiting for someone to make a fourth. Would you like to take his place?"

"I don't play cards."

"We'll explain the game to you."

"No, thanks."

There was still the same sneer on Théo's face, and he felt like punching it. But you couldn't strike a shrimp of a man like the hardware dealer. You even wondered how he managed to cope with his job.

Mimile pushed his full glass toward him.

"I see you've bought your brother a new tractor."

"Well, he works for me, doesn't he?"

"All the same, it must have cost you a pretty penny."

"It had to be got, didn't it?"

The rain had stopped, but the sky was overcast and the dark outline of the Île de Ré was invisible on the other side of the bay.

"Better that the bad weather should come at neap tide."

He kept seeing those two women ironing in the pleasant warmth of the kitchen. Was Alice more talkative with Jeanne? Did she feel more at ease than with a man?

He wanted to win her confidence. He had been wrong to come home drunk the night before. She must have noticed, and it was not the sort of thing to enhance his prestige.

But what did he care, really? He was a free man, surely? Nobody had ever ventured to tell him what to do and what not to do.

Not a grubby little chit of a girl . . .

He was vexed with himself, as if he had uttered a blasphemy. He poured himself a fresh glass and tossed it off.

85

"What do I owe you?"

He did not need to wait for the answer. It was the same sum every day.

"Come on, Doudou old fellow," he muttered, as if the deaf-mute were able to hear him.

Anyway, Doudou followed him.

He set to work again at the far end of the garden, for about an hour, and then went to wash his face and hands at the pump before sitting down at table for lunch.

CHAPTER 4

He had begun to drink heavily, as if that would stop him from thinking, and the more he drank the more he was haunted by the thought of Alice, who had assumed an ever-increasing importance in his mind.

If he had been told, only ten days earlier, that this would happen to him, he would have shrugged his shoulders. To other people, maybe. Not to him. He'd never been bowled over by any woman, not even his wife.

Jeanne's attitude, as it happened, was disconcerting. She displayed no uneasiness. She was as calm and cool as usual, with a certain unchanging stiffness. And yet she was watching him as one might watch an invalid, trying to understand the development of his illness.

When she surprised him in the kitchen for no ostensible reason, she behaved as though his presence there were quite natural, and it was he who was put out of countenance.

He reached the point where he could no longer look her in the face. It seemed to him that his features must surely betray his distress, and even at Mimile's he was glum, almost surly.

And Alice? Did she realize what was happening to him? She went about her business without appearing to notice anything and her face showed no expression.

Didn't she find it ridiculous that a man of his age should get into such a state on account of a chit like herself? Or was she, on the contrary, secretly flattered by it?

He did not know. He had stopped wanting to know. It hurt him to think. He felt confusedly that things could not go on like this, that one day or another he would make the gesture, and he felt ashamed of it beforehand, it frightened him.

On Thursday night, in bed, he listened to Jeanne's regular breathing. If she hadn't been there . . . He had been drinking, at Mimile's and at home. His thoughts were hazy and distorted. If Jeanne had not been there . . . If Jeanne were no longer there . . . If anything should happen to Jeanne . . .

She had high blood pressure and had already had two

heart attacks. The doctor had warned her to be careful. Supposing he should be left alone . . . Would he marry Alice?

People would laugh at him. A man of forty-five marrying a child of sixteen! Well, no matter; he didn't care. Yes, he would marry her, whatever might happen later.

Jeanne was far from imagining the thoughts that he was turning over in his mind, and next morning, as between half-closed eyelids he watched her getting up, he remembered his last night's obsessions.

He was unfair to her. Another woman would probably have made a scene. She, in spite of her clear-sightedness, said nothing to him, remained unmoved, without a sign of impatience or ill temper.

It was almost as though he were sickening for some illness. She seemed to be waiting for him to need her care.

It was another gray, gloomy day. He went to look at the restless sea, which was covered with whitecaps, and the low clouds, heavy with rain, scudding across the sky.

At Mimile's, Porchet was sneering as usual. Louis Cardis had resumed his place at the *belote* table, his right leg in a plaster cast and his crutches by his side.

Once more, Doudou followed his master like a big dog ready to bite anyone or anything that threatened him.

Lecoin was convinced that the deaf-mute knew. He might not be very bright, and he had never been taught anything. But just like dogs, he had an instinct that never misled him.

What did he think about what was happening? The strange thing was that what Lecoin dreaded most was disappointing the deaf-mute and losing his respect.

In the afternoon he suddenly decided to go on another spree. He was fed up with prowling about the house or around it in the hope of catching sight of a girl's skirt, of meeting her glance.

He was in a bad humor. As soon as he opened Nénette's door he saw her brow darken, but he did not care. She could think what she liked of him.

He sat down on a stool.

"Isn't anybody here?" he asked in surprise.

"The upstairs room's occupied."

"For a long time?"

"I don't expect so. You'll have a brandy, I suppose?"

Outside, it was raining and the atmosphere in the bar was gloomy.

"D'you know, it upsets me to see you like that?"

"Like what?"

"You know better than I do. You forget that I'm your old pal. How long have we known one another?"

"Some fifteen years."

"It was before I had my own bar, and I was a clumsy beginner trying to pick up clients. I looked so respectable and innocent in those days that men didn't dare approach me."

"It was on the Rue du Minage."

"Yes. One winter night. I'd decided to keep on trying for another quarter of an hour and then go back to bed, I was so cold. You came along and you looked at me in surprise. You passed me and then turned back. You walked past me again to have another look."

He remembered. She had been barely twenty, and she looked much younger still. Her lips had been pursed as if she'd wanted to cry.

"I was quite surprised when you spoke to me at last and asked me where I was going. I told you: home. And you said, quite calmly and softly:

" 'May I go with you?'

"You were a good-looking fellow. You still are. You often came back to see me. I had a little furnished room and the bedsprings creaked. Don't you remember the noise they made?"

He was listening inattentively, thinking that it might have happened that way with Alice.

"We didn't see one another for a long time, and then a shipowner who had fallen for me offered me this bar. You see I can honestly say we're old pals. I've seen all sorts in my time, you know.

"And I can tell right away when a man's eating his heart out. That's what you're doing right now."

"Another brandy."

"If you like. I realize you've come here to get drunk rather than for the girls, and that's not like you. You're in a bad way, my boy. And it can't be business worries. They say you're rolling in money."

He would have liked to make her shut up, but he hadn't the heart.

"Is it your wife?"

"No. She's just the same as ever. I've nothing against her."

He had once told Nénette that his wife was frigid and that making love was an ordeal for her. It was true. And that was probably why she had never been jealous.

"Your brother?"

"I've no reason to worry about him."

"You're not going to tell me you've fallen in love?"

The word touched him to the quick and he nearly flared up.

"It happens at any age, you know. I got it badly myself three years ago. It lasted for six months and I suffered a lot. And yet here I am, and it doesn't hurt any more."

They heard a door closing and steps on the stair. A man came down, with his coat collar turned up and his head lowered, and crossed the room hurriedly as though he were ashamed.

"Most of them are like that afterward."

A girl he had had the week before, the plump blonde, climbed onto a stool at the end of the bar.

Nénette would not drop the thread of the conversation.

"Won't she have you?"

"It's not that."

"It's somebody you can't touch?"

He did not reply. "Have you got a girl for me?"

With a glance, she indicated the one who had just come down.

"No, really! I'd feel I was putting on slippers still warm from someone else's feet."

"I'll try, but it's not easy."

She went into the back parlor and he heard her make three telephone calls.

The first time she said:

"All right, darling, can't be helped. Better luck next time. No, of course I forgive you."

She got no reply to the second call. Finally, the third time, she spoke at some length.

"You've merely got to take a taxi. Don't worry."

When she resumed her place at the counter he asked her:

"Who is it?"

"You don't know her. She's a dressmaker and she only comes from time to time. You'll have to make do with just one today."

He didn't care.

"Champagne, I suppose?"

"Yes."

That, or anything else! He didn't even know why he had come.

"Wait a minute while I tidy the room."

He nodded toward the girl at the end of the counter: "Give her a drink on me."

Then he waited, watching the rain fall. Soon a taxi stopped by the sidewalk and a young woman in a raincoat got out. After paying the driver, she came in, and seemed surprised not to find Nénette.

"She's upstairs," he explained. "She'll be down directly."

She clearly guessed that this was the man who was expecting her, and sat down on the stool next to him.

"What'll you drink?"

"A mint cordial with water."

He went around to the other side of the counter and served her, while she watched his actions in some astonishment.

"You're obviously an old customer."

"And you?"

"It's just a month since I came to La Rochelle. I've only been here once. I have a job."

"I know. You're a dressmaker."

"I used to live at Luçon. My husband left me. I had to find a job that wasn't too difficult."

Nénette came downstairs again.

"I see you've got to know each other already."

And to Lecoin: "Her name's Hélène."

Then, to the girl: "This is M. Victor, one of my best friends. He's feeling blue. Try to cheer him up. You can go upstairs, my dears. I'll bring you the champagne right away."

The young woman seemed ill at ease. She was wearing a dark green suit under her raincoat. She had a good figure and a pleasant face.

In the end they went upstairs, one behind the other. The room was gloomy, as though the fog pervaded it, and he went to pull the curtains and switch on the bedside lamp.

Nénette followed close on their heels and set the champagne and glasses on a small table.

"Do you often come here?" the girl asked.

He noticed that she did not immediately *tutoyer* him, as most of them did. There was a kind of reserve, of awkwardness, about her.

"It depends. At certain times."

"And do you always have champagne brought up?"

"Yes."

"You're fond of it?"

"Of that or of anything else. . . ."

"It's years since I've had any. Actually, not since my wedding."

"How long have you been married?"

"Three years. I had a stillborn baby. My husband had a good job, but he's unreliable. One fine day when I came home from shopping I found his things had vanished from the apartment. I don't know where he is. He's never given me any news of himself. In any case he's left Luçon and I imagine he's gone to Paris. He was always talking about it. He was ashamed of living in the provinces. And what about you? Do you live at La Rochelle?"

"No. A small village about eight miles away. Here's to your good health!"

He drank off two glasses in quick succession.

"Will you undress?"

"D'you really want me to?"

"Why do you ask?"

"Because you don't behave like a man who wants to make love."

Everyone guessed, even this woman whom he had never met until a quarter of an hour ago. Whether at home or at Mimile's or here, he seemed to be under a magnifying glass, and they were all trying to discover the real reasons for his behavior.

She undressed after all, and she had a really beautiful body and very white, soft skin.

"You're not disappointed?"

"No."

"Aren't you going to undress?"

"No."

He caressed her absently, thinking about Alice. Why had it happened with that particular girl? He could have had all the women he liked.

If he had fallen in love with someone else, he could have set her up in a nice little apartment and gone to see her two or three times a week, every day if he felt like it.

"What are you thinking about?"

"Nothing."

"Whom are you thinking about?"

"About a girl," he finally admitted.

"Can't you have her?"

"No."

"Why? Doesn't she want you?"

"I don't know."

They were lying side by side, and eventually she grew bolder and began to fondle him almost automatically.

"Is that why you come here?"

"I used to come here before."

"Nénette's a splendid woman. And yet she hasn't always had an easy time of it. She's had her ups and downs."

"I've known her for fifteen years."

He got up to have a drink. He was too clearheaded. He needed to make his thoughts a bit hazier. He brought a glass to his companion, who sipped it slowly, leaning on one elbow. She kept watching him as though trying to solve a problem.

"I haven't known many men," she admitted at last. "But I don't think there can be many like you. How long have you been like this?"

"A couple of weeks."

"And before that?"

"I was like anyone else."

"Try to stop thinking for a little while."

They made love quite simply and affectionately, and she enjoyed it more than he did.

"Have we finished?" she asked, as he got up.

"No. I want a drink."

"D'you always drink so much?"

She called him *tu* now.

"No."

The bottle was almost empty. He pressed the electric bell, which rang in the bar, and a few minutes later Nénette knocked at the door and came in with two bottles.

"I've brought you two at once."

And the young woman, on the bed, looked almost frightened.

"Are you going to drink all that?"

He merely shrugged his shoulders. She didn't know him. He filled her glass, but she only drank a third of it and put it down on the bedside table.

"What did you feel like when you found your husband had gone?"

"I don't know. At the beginning I felt lost. Then I thought perhaps it was for the best. We weren't suited to one another. He was excitable and scatterbrained, always concocting impossible plans, and I'm inclined to be calm and sensible. I didn't want to stay at Luçon, where I've got relatives, and so I came to La Rochelle. I've only found a few customers so far, but that'll improve. Meanwhile, I come here from time to time.

"I've never met anyone like you. Other men are uneasy, or else they tell you their life story. And afterward they're in a hurry to go away. But with you one has the impression of having known you for a long time. One wants to ask you questions, but I don't suppose you like that."

"No."

She emptied her glass.

"What d'you do, once you're tight?"

"Nothing. I go home."

"Doesn't your wife say anything?"

"No."

"You're a phenomenon."

"I'm an ordinary man. I want a drink. Give me your glass."

They finished the second bottle before he lay down beside her again.

A quarter of an hour later Nénette knocked discreetly at the door. He called out to her to come in. She beckoned to him.

"I've got another downstairs that you don't know. Shall I send her up?"

He hesitated.

"No."

Hélène and he were all right together. She didn't fuss. Now that she had had three or four drinks her eyes were sparkling and she laughed readily.

"What did she want?"

"To send me up somebody."

"Do you usually take several at a time?"

"Two or three. It depends on what turns up."

"Have you been doing this for a long time?"

"Yes and no. It used to be once a week or every two weeks. Right now, I'm quite capable of coming here every day."

"Shall we see one another again?"

"Probably."

"Would you like to have my address? Have you got anything to write on?"

He got his notebook out of his pocket.

"Hélène Fournot, 27 Rue du Marché, second floor. I never take people at home, but with you it's different. I shan't have any champagne to offer you but I'll buy a bottle of cognac and keep it for you. I saw you were drinking brandy when I came in. D'you think you'll come?"

"I expect so."

"You know, I won't charge you anything."

There was a certain naïveté about her.

"Don't tell Nénette, though, she'd resent it."

How unlike Alice it all was! It seemed as if all women were accessible and anxious to please him, except the little slattern from Surgères.

And what if he made love to Alice? Would she resist? Would she leave the house?

He opened the third bottle, drank a glassful, and lay down again.

"What shall we do?" asked Jeanne when they had finished breakfast.

"We'll go and eat somewhere, anywhere. Let's go to Niort. We haven't been there for a long time."

Alice was upstairs, dressing for Mass. It had stopped raining but the wind was strong and the sea rough.

Would she spend the whole afternoon walking along the shore again?

They dawdled, and it was half past ten when Victor took the Peugeot out of the garage. Instead of taking the direct route they made a long detour by Luçon, Fontenay-le-Comte, and Pouzauges.

They just drove for the sake of the drive, because they had nothing else to do and nothing to say to one another.

At Niort they went into the brasserie on the main square where they usually lunched, and Victor ordered his customary sauerkraut, while his wife just had a lamb chop.

There were other couples like themselves, some with children, taking advantage of their Sunday to lunch out. Lecoin usually came here when the fair was on, and then the room was crowded with men standing and sitting and the atmosphere was unbreathable.

They came home by a roundabout way so as to use up most of the afternoon. Lecoin kept expecting Jeanne to speak of Alice, to warn him, but she did no such thing. She wore an anxious look, but this was usual with her.

Just as they were entering the house at about five o'clock, the telephone bell rang in the office and Jeanne hurried to answer it.

"Hello . . . Hello, yes . . . It's me . . . Have you been ringing long? . . . The third time? . . . We'd gone to Niort. . . . What did you say? . . ."

Turning to her husband, she whispered:

"It's Bernard."

Bernard Bertaut, the husband of Hortense, Jeanne's elder sister. They lived at Cholet, in Maine-et-Loire, where Bertaut owned a textile mill. They had three grownup children. One daughter was married to a Parisian. The son, André, was in Canada, where he worked in radio and television. Only the younger of the daughters was still living at home.

"You're sure? . . . The doctors told you so? . . ."

She spoke haltingly, and she sat down as though her legs were giving way from emotion.

"Yes . . . I'll come, of course . . . No, I'll take the train . . . Victor may need the car while I'm away . . . I believe there's a train about half past six . . . Yes . . . I'll be with you soon . . . Courage, Bernard."

Bernard was a stout, rosy-faced man, usually smiling.

Jeanne was taking some time to recover her wits.

"She had a third operation yesterday. . . ."

Hortense was suffering from cancer of the uterus and had already been operated on twice during recent years.

"It seems the cancer's spread and the surgeons could do nothing but sew her up again. They think there's no hope."

"Poor woman."

"I'm going there, of course. Bernard's quite crushed. I could scarcely understand what he was saying."

"Why don't you take the car?"

"I told you. I don't know how long I'll be away. It

102

depends on Hortense's condition. You may need the car."

In any case she was not keen on driving, ever since a slight collision with a bus.

"I'm going to pack a small suitcase. In the meantime, would you check the time of the train on the timetable, which is behind my desk, on the top shelf?"

So he was going to be alone in the house with Alice. He could not quite get over it. He dared not feel any delight. Moreover, he did not know what would happen, he could make no plans.

"Six fifty-seven," he said, as he went into the bedroom.

"I don't know why, but ever since this morning I've felt something weighing on me. It was like a presentiment. My dear good Hortense, who is so proud of her children."

She was putting underwear, a dress, shoes, and toilet articles into the suitcase.

"Will you take me to the station?"

"Of course."

He carried the suitcase downstairs, and poured himself a big glass of wine and then another. His hands were shaking with nervous excitement. He had not foreseen that it would happen so quickly, that he was going to find himself quite alone with Alice.

He was eager for his wife to be gone, for he was afraid of her noticing his unease, if she had not already noticed it.

They met Alice returning on foot from the seashore.

"Have you nothing to tell her?" he asked.

"She knows what she's got to do."

They went on their way. At the station Jeanne made straight for the ticket office.

"All right. Don't bother waiting to see me off."

They kissed one another lightly on both cheeks as usual.

Then, just as he was about to go back to the car, she murmured almost reluctantly:

"Be careful, all the same, Victor."

Her words gave him a kind of shock because, for once, especially as she said his Christian name, there had been a tender note in her voice.

After all, they were really fond of one another, in their own way. They hadn't lived together all that time for nothing.

And she knew him so well! She was aware that he was vulnerable, and he realized this and was often irritated, even humiliated, by it. She tended to treat him like an overgrown, irresponsible child.

He stopped at a bar to have a brandy, hoping in this way to steady his shaking hands. Then he got back into the car, and a few minutes later drove it into the garage. He looked at his watch. The train had left by now.

He crossed the courtyard and went in through the kitchen, where Alice was busy beating eggs. She had already changed from her navy blue dress into her checked apron.

"Isn't Madame with you?"

"She's had to go to Cholet, where her sister is dying."

He watched her reactions. She said nothing. It seemed to him that her face grew a little graver, then she looked at him as though silently questioning him.

"What are you fixing for dinner?"

"Madame said an omelette. What sort would you like? With bacon?"

"That'll do."

He poured himself a drink.

"Would you like a glass?"

"I never drink. I don't like wine, and spirits even less."

"You're lucky."

He did not know what to do with himself. He went into the dining room, then into the living room, and then upstairs, where he left his jacket in the bedroom.

He was not as happy as he'd have expected Jeanne's absence to make him. It would probably last several days. She had promised to keep in touch by telephone.

It felt very odd to him to be sitting alone in the dining room with Alice serving him. Her face was still inscrutable. What was she thinking about? Was she wondering, as he was, what was going to happen?

She could not be unaware of the effect she had on him. Didn't she care? Was she frightened?

He ate rapidly, while she took her meal separately at a corner of the kitchen table.

"Are you afraid of me, Alice?"

"Why should I be afraid?"

"I don't know. Sometimes you seem to avoid me and you only speak to me when you have to."

"I'm always like that."

He longed to take her in his arms, but he would not do so. He watched television while she cleared the table, washed the dishes, and tidied up the kitchen.

A quarter of an hour later she peeped in, after knocking at the door, to ask if he needed her any more.

"Then I'll go up to bed."

"So will I."

He waited until she had reached the second floor before he went upstairs and into his bedroom. His throat was tight. His hands went on shaking while he undressed and put on his pajamas and slippers.

The room seemed so empty! He would never have believed that Jeanne filled such an important place in the house.

He got into bed and put out the light. Overhead, he heard Alice's footsteps as she moved to and fro, then a final sound, the bed moving on its casters as she lay down on it.

He clenched his teeth, saying to himself: "No! . . . No! . . ."

It made him dizzy, and a quarter of an hour later he switched on the bedside lamp, got up, and put on his dressing gown.

At the door, he hesitated again. He went up noise-

106

lessly, as though not to alarm her, and gently turned her door handle, but the bolt was fastened inside.

Then, holding his breath, he knocked. There was a fairly long pause.

"Who's there?" she asked at last.

"It's me."

"One moment."

Barefoot, a long nightgown over her thin body, she opened the door to him, and stood back to let him come in.

Without a word he put both arms around her waist and clasped her closely. Perhaps for a few seconds her body stiffened, but when he sought her lips she did not turn away. She just remained passive.

"You can't understand, Alice."

She was looking at him without surprise.

"For the last two weeks I haven't been myself. I don't know how I've managed to live. It's the first time in my life this has happened to me."

"I'm cold," she murmured, moving toward the bed and slipping under the covers.

"Are you afraid?"

"No."

Hadn't he already asked her that? He did not know. He had waited feverishly for this moment, and now that it had come he was disconcerted and did not know what to do.

"I'm not a brute, Alice."

She was looking at him with some curiosity, as if she had never seen a man in such an attitude. He came slowly toward the bed, as though to tame her, then he stroked her dark hair.

His hand slipped down to her shoulder and then, over her nightgown, lingered on her chest and her small breasts, still childlike.

She made no protest, did not repulse his hand. It moved farther down till it reached her private parts, when she gave a start.

Still very gently, he raised the nightgown, and now his fingers lay on the tiny triangle of black hair over her pubis.

He had dreamed of it too much. He had too often imagined this moment. He didn't know what he was doing. He slid between the covers beside her, and as they lay cheek to cheek and she felt his organ against hers she whispered:

"You won't hurt me?"

He discovered that she was a virgin, and the blood rushed to his head. He did not know if what he felt was joy or vexation.

Jeanne had warned him, but it was too late. Jeanne was now traveling toward Cholet, while he, little by little, slowly, clasping the girl tight to reassure her, was pressing into her.

"In a few moments you won't feel anything."

"It hurts."

"You'll see it'll soon be over."

He had to withdraw almost immediately, for he was about to come.

"Was it really painful?"

"Not very."

"Next time, you'll just enjoy it."

She made no reply. Slowly, he stroked her whole body, and he took hold of her hand.

Was it just resignation? He would have liked to talk openly to her. Above all he would have liked to have her talk to him, but her face remained expressionless, and so did her eyes, staring at him from close up.

"I love you very much, Alice. You can't understand. You're too young."

It distressed him to feel her so remote, apparently indifferent.

"Are you a little fond of me?"

She kept silence for a while before whispering: "I don't know."

"You're not afraid of me any more?"

"No."

"I'm going to let you go to sleep. Good night, Alice."

He kissed her but met only the tips of her lips.

"Good night," he repeated, slipping out of the bed.

He put on his dressing gown and slippers again and made for the door.

"Till tomorrow."

He wanted to cry, without quite knowing why. He was

overflowing with tenderness. His passion for Alice was not merely sexual, he had just proved this to himself. He would have liked to . . .

To do what? To clasp her to him even tighter, as though to choke her. To melt into her. To be fused with her. To feel her belonging to him, to him alone, happy and trustful.

He went down the two floors and poured himself a glass of brandy. His legs were weak with emotion. He felt rather ashamed of this: it was unlike him.

"Alice!" he murmured, like an incantation.

She was not beautiful. Her body was unfinished and angular. She lay unresponsive in his arms and tightened her lips when he kissed her.

He would have to win her confidence. He felt happy and miserable both at once.

It had happened at last. And she herself, knowing he was on the landing, had drawn back the bolt of her attic door. And yet she must have known what he had come for.

So then?

He could not understand her. He tried to find an explanation. She had been passive, nothing more, and her voice had only betrayed a certain emotion when she had whispered, very low:

"You won't hurt me?"

He poured himself a second glass and went to sit down in an armchair in the living room, for he felt unable to go to sleep yet.

When she came back Jeanne would quickly realize what had happened. She would merely have to look at him.

Would she reproach him? Or would she pretend to know nothing about it?

He remembered Théo's sneering laugh and the allusions he had made even before Lecoin was aware of Alice's arrival.

What the hardware dealer had not foreseen was that Lecoin would fall foolishly and naïvely in love. Nénette, on the other hand, had understood, and it had distressed her, as if nothing good could come of it.

He was forty-five. All his life he had worked hard, and although Jeanne had done her best to help him there had never been any emotional relationship between them.

He had gone after women with a kind of fury, as if to prove something to himself.

To prove what?

And now at last he was experiencing love, or something very much like it.

He wanted to go upstairs again, not to embrace Alice but to talk to her. He would have liked her to understand. He needed to know that she had not merely submitted to him, as to the farmer at Surgères.

He had imagined that after what had just happened he would be beside himself with joy, or that at least he would get some satisfaction from the memory of his pleasure. But on the contrary he now felt an even greater distress, because all sorts of questions beset him.

He would have liked to confide in someone, and if his wife had been there he might perhaps have talked frankly to her. Hitherto she had always understood him. Why should she not understand the whole thing?

He emptied his glass, put the bottle back in the corner cupboard, and switched off the light in the living room.

In his bedroom he felt more alone than ever, and he almost got dressed again to drive over to La Rochelle, where he would be in touch with people and hear the sound of voices.

The silence of the house oppressed him. He went to bed none the less, but it was a good half hour before he fell asleep.

Next day there was a fuller tide and things would be busy at the mussel beds again. He went downstairs in his working clothes and found Alice in the kitchen, making his coffee.

He looked in vain on her face or in her eyes for any trace of what had happened the night before.

"Did you sleep well?" he asked her.

He dared not say *tu* as he had done to all the other servants they had had, although she was the youngest of them all.

She nodded.

"Will you be having eggs?"

"Yes. Boiled, this morning."

He dared not kiss her. In any case they could have been seen from the courtyard. Doudou must be somewhere around the house. It was true that Doudou was undoubtedly more aware of the situation than Jeanne.

He knew everything that happened, not only in the house but in the village, and when he wanted to make himself understood, he could find the most expressive gestures.

"Thank you, Alice. Stay here a moment while I eat. I didn't sleep much last night. That shouldn't surprise you. You see, what I'd like is for you to feel convinced that I'm sincere. I'm not trying to take advantage of you. These last two weeks I've tried not to think about you. I went to La Rochelle to get drunk and find women, hoping that would stop me from thinking of you."

Perhaps, though he couldn't be certain, the ghost of a smile flitted across the girl's lips.

"All I'm telling you is the truth. I want you to believe me and feel a little bit fond of me."

She said nothing. She had not sat down. She was standing between the table and the kitchen door.

"You don't hate me for it? You're sure?"

"I don't hate you for it."

Unfortunately, she added, as though making an obvious comment:

"You're a man. . . ."

That was all he had got out of her! A man, like that swine of a Paquot, presumably. And hadn't he, after all, behaved in the same way? He had even gone much further.

If she were to tell what had happened the previous night, he might be arrested and spend two years in prison.

"I'm not just a man. I'm a man in love."

He rose clumsily and went toward her, holding out his hand.

"Give me your hand."

She hesitated, and finally did so.

"Friends?"

She answered only with an uncertain sort of nod.

"I'll be seeing you presently. I'm going to work at the mussel beds."

He went to join Doudou, who was loading the empty hampers onto the two trucks, and sat down heavily at the wheel.

CHAPTER 5

Back among the colorful scenes at the mussel beds, he threw himself into his work with a kind of fury, but in vain: Alice had somehow invaded his very body. He could not think about anything else.

Their last night's intimacy, if it could be called that, had not cured him. On the contrary, it had left him feeling unsatisfied. He wanted something more, he could not have said exactly what.

A total fusion. Something he had known neither with Jeanne nor with any other woman.

He thought about her all the time. He would say to himself:

"Just now, she's tidying the bedroom."

And he would have liked to be there with her, looking at her, watching all her movements. He would have liked her to look at him from time to time with the trustful glance of an accomplice.

He was suddenly aware that he had always been a lonely man. Jeanne lived with him, worked with him. She was an associate. He could not even say that they were good friends. On the contrary, he had always borne her a slight grudge for guessing his thoughts.

At heart, he still regarded her as a schoolmistress. And he even resented her indulgence. He would have preferred an open row which would have allowed him to tell her what he really felt.

But why Alice? Why that young thing, who went about the house as though she did not belong to it, and who even in his arms remained indifferent and remote?

What did she think of him? Did she think at all? Was she intelligent?

He knew nothing, whereas he would have liked to know all about her, to possess her really. He would have liked the two of them to be as one.

He had lived forty-five years without such an idea ever occurring to him, and he would have laughed at anyone who behaved as he was doing.

He wondered what he would say to her when he went home. He had so much to say to her! He felt sure she was mistaken about him, that she thought of him as a man like all other men, merely wanting to take advantage of her.

That was not true. He loved her. That word, which was not part of his usual vocabulary, was enough to set his cheeks aflame.

He did not want to lose her. Above all, she mustn't leave. He would keep her from going. She would come to understand.

The tide still covered part of the mussel beds and he only loaded some thirty hampers, including his own, into the truck.

He had the impression that everyone was watching him, some with pity, others with irony. Nobody had expected this of him. He had always been taken for a self-sufficient man, a sort of rogue animal with nothing but contempt for all around him.

Well, now they realized that it was not true, that he was as vulnerable as the rest.

He wondered how his father had lived since his wife's death, nearly forty years ago. He had had practically no contact with anyone, except Daniel and his wife. Even so, when they sat together at mealtimes he never spoke a word. He followed his routine, with a faraway look in his eyes, and he had never confided in anyone.

Lecoin went on to Charron, where he collected only a few hampers, and here too he felt that everyone was watching him.

He almost went home without stopping at Mimile's,

but he wanted to keep up his tradition. Doudou followed him, as usual, and it struck him that the expression in the deaf-mute's eyes was not quite the same as on other days.

While Mimile served him his drink, Théo addressed him brazenly.

"So your wife's away?"

Someone must have seen them both at the station at La Rochelle.

"The coast is clear now, eh? You'll be able to enjoy yourself."

They were all watching him, sniggering and yet ill at ease. Everyone knew that his rages were terrible. He knew it, too. He mistrusted his own impulses.

Doudou sat tense, ready to spring; Lecoin, his fists clenched, signaled to him to keep still. He himself remained motionless, his eyes fixed on Théo's.

The latter, somewhat alarmed, muttered:

"You know, you mustn't mind what I say. . . ."

"I'd advise you not to go on."

He had such a threatening look and was obviously restraining himself with such difficulty that the little man gave way.

"After all, Chief, it's none of my business. People can enjoy themselves however they want to."

It seemed as if everyone knew what had happened the night before, and he hated the whole lot of them. He hated the whole village for besmirching his love.

"Don't pay any attention to him," Mimile advised in

an undertone, leaning over the counter. "He's a poor creature."

"A poor creature who'd better keep his mouth shut unless he wants me to wring his neck."

He calmed down a little as he drank his wine, but his nerves were still on edge. When he got home Alice was in the kitchen, stirring something in a saucepan with a wooden spoon.

"Is it half past twelve already?" she asked in surprise.

"No. Ten past. You've plenty of time. What's that you're making?"

"A lamb stew."

"So you know how to cook."

He had just used *tu* inadvertently, and he went on doing so. It was some slight progress toward intimacy.

"A bit."

"You know, Alice . . ."

She was looking at him, waiting for him to go on, and he hunted in vain for the words he would have liked to utter.

"What I feel for you is something very serious. Last night you may have thought I was behaving like a brute."

She shook her head.

"I so much want you to understand me. Come and kiss me, will you?"

She came up to him, still holding the wooden spoon, and lifted her face, but without parting her lips.

"You'll stay here?"

"If you and Madame keep me."

"Madame has no reason not to keep you. There's no sort of bond between us."

"She's your wife."

"On paper. We live in the same house, we sleep in the same room, but there's no bond between us."

She returned to her stew, and he felt he had gone about things badly. Had anyone, hitherto, tried to understand her and shown any real interest in her?

Wasn't it natural that she should think he, Lecoin, had merely been bent on his own pleasure?

"Does it still hurt?"

"A little."

"That'll soon pass. You're a real woman now."

The telephone rang in the office. He went to lift the receiver.

"This is Jeanne," said a voice at the other end of the line.

"Yes. How is your sister?"

"Very bad. There's nothing that can save her now or keep her going much longer. They're giving her as much morphia as she wants."

"Is she aware of it?"

"She's terribly lucid. She said to me this morning: 'If only it doesn't last much longer. I'd rather go off without too much pain. It's my poor husband I'm worrying about. He's never lived alone all his life.'

"Her daughter Jeanine has come from Paris. There are almost too many of us here, and she's in a tiny room at the hospital. I had a word in the corridor with the doctor who's treating her."

"What does he say?"

"That she may last three or four days, a week at most. Apparently when they hand out morphia so freely it means the end is near."

Jeanne's voice sounded weary.

"Have you been able to sleep?"

"No. I've been sitting up with her. Bernard is worn out and he seems to have aged ten years since the last time I saw him."

She broke off to ask: "And you?"

"Everything's as usual. This morning I went back to the mussel beds."

"Is Alice looking after you all right?"

"Yes."

"What's she giving you to eat today?"

"Lamb stew."

"One of these days you'll have to come over for the funeral. I don't like having to talk like this but one must face facts."

"I'll come, of course."

"I'll keep you informed. Take care of yourself."

He went back to the dining room, where his place was set, and Alice promptly came over to serve him.

"That was Madame. Her sister is dying. One of these days I'll have to go to Cholet for the funeral. I'll leave early with the car and I'll be back the same evening."

She showed neither pleasure nor anxiety.

121

"Didn't Madame say anything?"

"About what?"

"About our being alone in the house."

"She doesn't worry about that. She's not jealous. I've already told you."

He patted her affectionately on the buttocks while she waited on him, and she made no protest.

Nevertheless his thoughts now dwelt on Jeanne's more or less imminent return. It was true that she was not jealous, but would he dare, once she was back, to go up to Alice's room on the second floor?

He would be obliged to hide, to take advantage of the afternoons she went over to La Rochelle to shop.

When the mussels were washed and loaded onto the truck, Doudou went along with him to the station. They filled in the customary forms. Afterward, Lecoin was tempted to stop at Nénette's, not for the usual purpose but, on the contrary, to tell her triumphantly that he had no further need for her girls.

Triumphantly? He would have liked to believe it. He needed to keep telling himself that he was happy, even though he had never been so anxious in his life.

He wanted not to lose her. He wanted nobody to rob him of the least part of their slender intimacy.

It was at Mimile's that he finally drew up. A game of *manille* was in progress. Dr. Bourseau was there, his eyes a little bloodshot as usual. There were white threads nowadays in his short reddish beard. How old might he be? It seemed to Victor that he had always known him looking like that. When he was a child it was Dr. Bourseau who had looked after him and who had looked after his mother too.

In those days the doctor did not drink, and it was unusual to see him playing cards at Mimile's. His practice included three villages, Nieul, Marsilly, and Esnandes, and there were some weeks when he was wakened almost every night for a confinement.

Five or six years ago he had lost his wife, and he lived alone with a housekeeper who must have been about fifty. She had always been in love with him and now she shared his bed.

He drank far too much. Some people mistrusted him and went to La Rochelle for medical care, because his hands shook so. There was always a cigarette, which had usually gone out, hanging from his lips, and a small patch of his mustache and beard were stained yellow.

"What's new with you, Victor?"

"Nothing. My wife's gone to Cholet."

"So I've just heard. It seems her sister is dying?"

"She called me at noon. They're expecting the end any minute."

"Cancer, eh?"

"Yes."

"You're managing by yourself?"

"Yes."

He did not mention Alice, but it was understood.

When he got home, Alice was busy turning up the hem of an apron that was too long for her.

"You haven't been bored?"

"Why should I be bored?"

"Did you think of me a little?"

"I don't know. I did my work."

"Wouldn't you like us to go upstairs together?"

"Not now. I've got to see to the dinner."

This was a little better. Instead of her earlier monosyllabic answers she was speaking in real sentences, and she looked him in the eyes, calmly, without embarrassment or fear.

"I'm going to take off my boots and jersey and I'll be back," he told her.

He had just eaten three grilled herrings when the telephone rang. It was Jeanne again. Her voice was even fainter than in the morning.

"She's dead, Victor. Really, I'm glad of it for her sake, for she was in too much pain and she was praying to be released as quickly as possible."

"Were you with her?"

"Yes. Luckily, Bernard was not at her bedside. We'd got him to go home for a brief rest, because he was really at the end of his tether."

"Did she say anything?"

"Her lips moved, but no sound came out of them. Oddly, instead of holding her daughters' hands—they were both there—it was my hand that she had grasped and seemed to cling to."

"The funeral's to be on Thursday, at ten. Can you be here?"

"Of course."

"I'll probably come home with you."

"I'll have the car."

"I'll say good night right away, because I haven't the heart to go on talking for long. Hortense was my favorite."

For him, all this was remote and almost unreal. He was conscious only of the fact that he had just three more days alone with Alice. As on the night before, he waited until she had finished washing up and getting everything orderly.

He went up the stairs behind her and paused on the first floor.

"Alice."

"Yes?"

"Why shouldn't you spend the night here?"

"No. Not in Madame's room."

"It's my room too."

"It's not the same thing."

"As you like. I'll come up right away."

He took a shower and put on his pajamas and dressing gown. He still felt just as anxious, as though he did not quite believe in the reality of what was happening to him. He heard the sound of water splashing in the room above. She must be bathing too, in the washtub, as his mother used to bathe him when he was a child.

He avoided going up too soon and rolled a cigarette.

He was trying not to think of the future, for there seemed to be no way out.

Why shouldn't he go off with Alice? He would leave Jeanne enough money to live on. He would sell his land. He would let her keep the house and the mussel beds. He would even leave her in charge of the deaf-mute.

He felt ashamed of abandoning Doudou so, but it would be practically impossible to uproot him.

Where should he go? He hadn't the slightest idea. Not to Paris, in any case, for there he would not have the same sense of intimacy with Alice.

To the Midi, perhaps? He would buy a house and a small plot of land somewhere in the heart of the country.

He knew it would never happen. It seemed too easy. In reality, it would mean becoming a different man overnight, with different gestures and words and other roots. He belonged here, and he would probably be incapable of living anywhere else.

He put out his cigarette and went upstairs. She was in her nightgown, standing in front of a small bamboo-framed mirror combing her hair. He watched her, eager to clasp her to him. Meanwhile she was looking at him in the mirror and he had the impression, as he had had once before, that she was trying to smile at him.

When she laid down the comb he took her in his arms, lifted her up, and carried her to the foot of the bed.

"Take off your nightgown, will you?"

"Not with the light on."

"I'll put it out. Now take it off and lie down. . . ."

The switch was by the door, and he turned off the light. The unseen moon nevertheless shed a faint glow through the attic.

He had taken off his pajamas. He, too, was naked. He slipped in beside her.

"At last!" he sighed. He had been waiting for this moment all day.

"You're not afraid any more?"

"No. Just a tiny bit."

"I won't hurt you this time. You need only let yourself go."

He stroked her whole body slowly, lovingly. She was very thin, but he did not care. As his eyes grew accustomed to the semidarkness he could vaguely see her face, and he tried to make out its expression.

"I'm not making you unhappy?"

"No."

"Happy?"

"I don't know."

At any rate, she was trying to be nice to him, for she returned his caresses, unasked, with a timid hand.

"You see, I can't hope for you to love me as I love you. I just want you to feel a little fondness. You understand? And to begin with, I want you to realize that I'm your friend."

She whispered: "Yes."

"D'you think that's going to happen?"

And again the familiar words: "I don't know."

127

This time, her body suddenly quivered under his caress.

"Relax. Let yourself go completely."

For he felt her stiffening again.

"I'd like to stay with you always, day and night."

Her eyes were wide open, he could see despite the half-darkness, and she was staring up at the ceiling.

He spent a long time trying to soften her. Little by little, she became less tense.

She was only frightened for one brief moment, when he went into her, but he did it so gently that she relaxed once more. He stayed in her without moving. He stroked her hair.

"I love you, Alice."

He had never said that to any woman.

"I so much want you to be happy."

She quivered once again. It seemed as if her body was slowly beginning to awake.

He forced himself to wait without moving. He went a little deeper into her and when he felt that she was ready, he moved.

Then she clutched his arm almost feverishly. He knew what was happening. He wanted at all costs to restrain himself till the end, and at last she uttered a muffled cry.

Her whole body stiffened and then went limp in his arms.

"It didn't hurt you, did it?"

"No."

He kissed her on the mouth, and for the first time she parted her lips.

And, only then, he withdrew.

He lay on his back, with one hand on Alice's naked belly, in the attic over which the moon shed a diffused radiance. He seemed to be talking to himself, with an occasional long silence during which each of them could hear the other's heart beating.

"You know, I had a hard time too when I was young, and I've been very poor."

He was telling his own story, in fragments, a thing he had never done in his life before.

"When my mother died after giving birth to my brother Daniel I was just five years old. My father was a farm laborer. He couldn't look after us. So he put us to board with an old woman in Marsilly whom everybody called La Tati.

"She seemed to me old at the time, but in fact she can't have been more than about sixty. She lived in a tiny house at the end of a lane, which has since been destroyed in a fire.

"She was probably not such a bad creature, but I hated her and I used to think she smelled nasty.

"Father used to come and see us on Sundays, in the fine black suit he had worn for his wedding."

He recalled La Tati, who was a little like Jeanne twenty years older. She had the same square build, pale complexion, and strong hands.

This was the first time he had made any connection between the two women who, until the last few days, had mattered in his life.

He tried to find the word that suited them and would serve to describe them. Austerity? Strictness? Something of the sort. La Tati had recently been widowed and left destitute; she had taken the two children as boarders, and furthermore took in sewing for the women of the village.

She was said to be miserly, and it was true that at mealtimes they were given scanty helpings.

"I had to wait until I earned my own living to wear new clothes. Ours were made out of the neighbors' old clothes, or her late husband's.

"I realize now that she earned very little and could not have done otherwise.

"At school I was the tallest and the strongest, but I was also the most poverty-stricken. I wasn't at the bottom of the class, but I was not a very good scholar either, and whenever I was free I used to tend cattle to earn a little money."

Was she listening? Did it bore her to have him tell his life story? Wasn't it better that she should know him, so as not to have any mistaken ideas about him?

He indulged in no self-pity. Everything he said was quite true.

"In summer I watched my schoolfellows eating ices. Sometimes they offered me some and I said I didn't like them. Were you good at school?"

"Fairly good."

"Did you get your diploma?"

"Yes."

"I never did. My brother Daniel got his. At thirteen I left school and took a job on a farm, where I did a man's work. It's true that people who didn't know me took me for sixteen or seventeen.

"I'd already determined that I would get rich. I didn't know exactly what that meant. An old gentleman lived in this very house, which I admired greatly, and I often saw him sitting by the window, reading a thick book.

"And then there was the farmer for whom I worked. The farm belonged to an attorney from La Rochelle, to whom we used to take what was owing to him every month. It was Four Winds Farm; it belongs to me now and I've settled my brother there. Last Sunday you were quite close to it when you walked along the shore. It's the last farm before you get to Esnandes."

Then he had proof that she was listening to him.

"D'you own it?"

"Yes, and other properties too. I've got some land at Charron, which I lease to a butcher who puts his cattle out to graze there."

Their warm bodies were touching, in a kind of mutual trustfulness. She did not repulse his hand, which now lay close to the most secret part of her.

"My boss carried an old wallet in the back pocket of his trousers, and when he had to pay anyone you saw a big wad of notes.

"Maybe that's why I never get a new wallet, although mine is so worn. I feel safer, having plenty of money in my pocket and knowing that there's more at home. It's not like having it in a bank."

He had gone with girls since he was fifteen, but he did not mention that. Not that he wanted to conceal the fact, but because it never entered his mind. He had been to bed with women whom he could not even remember.

He attached no importance to the matter. He took his pleasure, and then he forgot. And if he pursued it so assiduously, wasn't it in order to gain self-confidence?

"I put aside almost everything I earned and I never showed my face in the bistrot.

"I was twenty-two when Hector Muflin, the tenant farmer of Four Winds, was killed by a kick from a horse. His wife and three children couldn't go on running the farm.

"I went to see the attorney at La Rochelle.

" 'I've heard a lot of good of you and I see you're a tough fellow. Are you married?'

" 'Not yet.'

" 'Are you planning to get married soon?'

" 'When I've found the right woman.'

"He laughed. He told me to come back two days later for his answer. I told him I would keep on Hector's wife and children until I got married.

"He accepted, and so that's what I did. The woman was a good soul, but ugly, and she was cross-eyed in the bargain. But she worked like a horse.

132

"We got on well together. In those days we didn't have all the machinery they have nowadays and the work was much harder. You had to take on day laborers, and get up at half past four even in winter to milk the cows by hand before the dairyman came around to collect the cans.

" 'Are you going to stay a bachelor for long?'

" 'I don't know. I shall see.'

"And then I met the schoolmistress from Nieul-sur-Mer, whom I'd only seen at a distance. It was at a charity fête. She was dressed in black and looked very respectable. She seemed more like a city person than a country person.

"She wasn't what you'd call pretty. She wasn't beautiful either, but she was nice to look at and you felt you could trust her.

"We danced together. Then, since it was very warm, we went for a walk outside.

" 'Are you from La Rochelle?'

" 'No. From Bressuire, in Deux-Sèvres.'

" 'I know the place. Would you like to live in the country?'

" 'Teaching in a school?'

" 'No. Living on a farm. . . .' "

He was smiling in the half-darkness.

"I'd made up my mind already, I don't know why. I didn't speak to her about it right away, but a month later I asked her to marry me. She was three years older than me, but I didn't mind."

"Did you love her?" Alice asked gently.

"No. I didn't know that at the time, but I do now. I was impressed because she was educated and behaved like a city person.

"I felt like a lout beside her and I was grateful when, a week or two later, she agreed to marry me.

"I had to go to Bressuire to meet her family. That's where the wedding took place.

"I had to go home the same day because of the farm. I meant to keep on Hector's widow for a while to give my wife a chance to get used to things, but to my surprise she took to it immediately.

"You'd have thought she had milked cows all her life, and she used a pitchfork like a man and cheerfully pushed along barrows of manure."

He was proud of her, just as he was proud of his herds, his lands, of everything that was his or was connected with himself.

He retained an extremely vivid memory of this period, and it seemed very close. He could scarcely believe that so many years had gone by.

He had become a mature man. He would soon seem an old one to the younger generation.

And yet he had scarcely lived.

"My brother tried to be a traveling salesman. He traveled for a firm that sold agricultural products, but in fact he spent more time in bistrots with his so-called customers than going from farm to farm.

"He took a clerk's job in La Rochelle but he stayed only a couple of months because he said he couldn't breathe in an office.

"I don't know how many jobs he tried. I sent for my father, who in spite of his age was as good as any tough laborer.

"Hector's widow had gone to live with relatives near Rochefort. I've met her two or three times since. She's aged a great deal."

He wanted to tell her the slightest details, so that she could share his life a little, but he was afraid of boring her by talking only of himself.

"Now I've come to the most important part. I thought I had married a real woman. During the first month I said to myself that she would gradually become one, and then I was forced to realize that she was frigid."

"What does that mean?"

"That she got no pleasure from making love. On the contrary, she disliked it.

"That was when I began visiting the prostitutes at La Rochelle from time to time."

She asked: "Is that why you don't love her any more?"

"No. Really, I've never been in love with her. I liked her. I enjoyed her company. She did her share of the work and she did it well. She never tried to deprive me of my freedom."

"She's not jealous?"

"Not at all."

"Last week . . ." she began.

As she stopped short, he encouraged her.

"Yes. Tell me what's on the tip of your tongue."

"You came back a couple of times rather . . . rather . . ."

"Drunk. You mustn't be afraid of words."

"Had you been visiting prostitutes, as you said?"

"Yes. Because of you."

"Why because of me?"

"I wanted dreadfully to hold you in my arms. I kept hanging around you and I thought of you all day long. I wanted to take my mind off you, but it didn't work."

"It was only when your wife had gone away," she murmured.

"Because I didn't want to take you in a hole-and-corner way."

"I think I understand. And when she comes back?"

"I don't suppose I shall announce to her that I'm going up to your room. She suspects it, in any case. She understood right away, possibly before I did myself, that I loved you. And did you?"

"I thought you wanted to fondle me and perhaps a bit more."

They fell silent. Then by degrees they began breathing faster, and presently he slipped into her. He had never realized the almost solemn character of this act. He performed it slowly, trying to read in her eyes.

This time she moaned almost immediately, a continuous muffled moaning that betrayed her pleasure.

"There's no risk of my having a baby?" she asked when he had withdrawn.

"No. I've taken care."

She just said: "Oh!" But in fact she probably did not know what he meant.

"Don't you think it's getting late?"

"I don't know what the time is, but it's true that you ought to get some sleep."

He gave her a long kiss in which there was gratitude as well as passion.

"You can't imagine the importance of what you've given me."

He did not switch on the light, and as he went downstairs he heard her bolt the door behind him.

As on the previous night, he went down to the ground floor. Once again, he poured himself a glass of brandy, put on the light in the living room, and sat for a while in an armchair.

He had experienced so much that evening that he felt the need to go over it all in his mind. It was a kind of climax to that whole life which he had been relating piecemeal.

He had never before confided in anyone. He himself rarely thought of the past. He was anxious that Alice should know him and should not misunderstand him.

He had wanted to become rich, at any rate rich in

137

comparison with the other inhabitants of Marsilly and Esnandes. He had succeeded by dint of ruthlessness toward himself and others.

He had to take his revenge on his own youth. He had been obliged to look after his brother, who otherwise would probably have come to a bad end. It was he, too, who nearly fifteen years earlier had taken charge of the deaf-mute. The latter had conceived a fierce affection for him, closer to the devotion of a great dog than to any human feeling.

He followed Lecoin everywhere, barefoot, and even when they were not together he guessed what his master was doing.

He had a kind of instinct that was rather mysterious. Almost always he anticipated his master's wishes, and then his wide mouth grew even wider in a blissful smile.

He seemed to say: "I've caught you out again!"

But he was capable of violent impulses, of blind rages, as he had proved once again when he had wanted to rush at Théo. He did not know his own strength, especially that of his great gnarled hands, which were like a gorilla's.

He seldom set foot in the house. At most, he would venture into the kitchen to bring in some oysters, or whatever parcel had been entrusted to him.

For him, Jeanne did not exist. She had no place in his little world. Perhaps he had understood that she was not really a wife to Lecoin but a sort of clerk who worked in his office.

What did he think now about Alice and about Lecoin's feelings for her? He had evidently guessed, and Lecoin wondered if he was jealous of her.

It was impossible to tell. He was like a blank wall.

Lecoin had mentioned none of this to Alice. He had not had time. The evening had left him with a pleasant sense of well-being and warmth. It seemed to him that he had taken an important step forward and had won her trust at last.

She had talked. She had even asked two or three questions. And finally, above all, her senses had been aroused, and making love no longer seemed to her an irksome task.

What worried her—and worried him too—was the prospect of Jeanne's return with him on Thursday evening, immediately after the funeral. He did not want to think of it too much, lest it should spoil his happiness, but it remained a serious problem in the background.

He poured himself another glass. She must have gone to sleep now, up there. He would have liked to sleep beside her, and he hoped she would consent to this someday.

At last he went up to bed. When he lay down he recognized Alice's odor on his own skin and breathed it in eagerly.

"Good night, little girl," he whispered.

He sank into sleep immediately, and when he opened his eyes it was time to get up. The low tide came very early. He had a quick breakfast, looking at the girl with a smile in his eyes.

"Happy?"

"Yes."

"Did you sleep well?"

"Yes."

She looked a little pale and weary, none the less.

"One of these days I'll take you along to the mussel beds."

She answered yes to whatever he suggested, but she was possibly not quite convinced that it would really take place.

He kissed her before leaving, and joined Doudou in the garage. They sat down side by side in the front of the truck.

"Morning, Doudou. We're going to have a sunny day."

He knew that the deaf-mute could hear nothing, but he talked to him none the less, for Doudou could read the words on his lips.

He pointed to the sky and then his hands sketched a circle in the air to represent the sun.

Lecoin was happy. He could not remember ever feeling so relaxed in his life, and he put off thinking about all his problems until later.

Why should he not tell Jeanne quite frankly what was happening? There was an empty room on the first floor, opposite their bedroom, which was used to store fruit. He could make that into a bedroom for Alice and himself.

It was simple. It was natural. Wasn't it better than going with prostitutes in La Rochelle or sleeping with some village woman and running the risk of being caught by a jealous husband?

It was too simple, obviously! She was Mme Lecoin, and even if that were only a fiction, it was a fiction that she valued.

"Doudou, old boy, how complicated life is!"

The deaf-mute nodded, as if that were his opinion too, but he promptly recovered his good humor at the sight of the mussel beds, where they were going to work while the sun appeared and rose slowly in the sky.

Today the sea was smooth and shining with just a slight whispering rim of foam at the very edge.

CHAPTER 6

Each morning, while he was at the mussel beds with the deaf-mute, she went out to do the marketing. She had quickly become familiar with the few shops in Marsilly, and everybody looked at her curiously when she went from one to the other with her shopping bag, thin and long-legged, her face impassive.

As for Victor Lecoin, he became increasingly humble toward her, sensitive to her least frown or even to an involuntary pout. He would ask her several times a day:

"Are you happy?"

He had the impression that she looked at him with a

certain impatience, a kind of irritation, and she would reply evasively:

"I think so."

Or else: "Why shouldn't I be?"

Her impassivity frightened him. It was hard to discern any sort of feeling in her face, which seemed to have become permanently inscrutable. She did what she had to do as best she could, but without any trace of zest or enthusiasm.

In the morning he would go into the kitchen to kiss her, and he was always disappointed by her apparent indifference.

"Your breakfast is ready."

Her lips remained tight shut under his own. She seemed to mistrust these repeated demonstrations of affection.

He told himself that she had never been used to such things, that he must allow her time to lose her shyness, and he waited impatiently for night to come, for then he had at least the illusion that she drew a little closer to him.

His visit to the second floor had become a rite. She no longer bolted her door, and on Tuesday he had found her crouching in the tub of soapy water.

This was a step forward in their intimacy. She had not attempted to cover herself with the towel. She had gone on washing while he rolled a cigarette.

Only one more day: Wednesday. And after that? He would go to Cholet for the funeral. He would come back, with his wife, who would resume her place in the double bed.

He did not want to think about it. He lived from day to day, from hour to hour, with sudden moments of anguish as though the future frightened him.

Théo still sniggered when he went to Mimile's. It was a mania of his. He had been like that as a schoolboy, when only his weakness saved him from being beaten up. He was always sour and crabbed.

"Don't pay any attention. He's a poor creature."

A poor creature and an unlovable one, who envied everyone else. He had had a very strict father who shut him up in a room until he had finished his homework and learned his lessons. The father was dead now. The mother was an invalid who still lived over the shop, in a dark room, where Théo's wife looked after her and brought up her meals.

She wasn't quite right in the head, people said. Passersby caught sight of a pallid face behind the windowpane. Her only entertainment consisted in watching people go by.

That Wednesday, Lecoin was sitting by himself at the table, and Alice was eating in the kitchen, when the telephone bell rang. He hurried into the office. He knew beforehand that it was his wife. He wondered what she wanted.

"Were you eating?"

"Yes."

"I'm sorry, but I was afraid I might miss you if I

144

called at a different time. It's going to be a very big funeral. The workshop will be closed and all the staff will be there. All the important people in Cholet, who are friends of Bernard's, will be there too.

"The mortuary chamber has been set up already. Her daughter-in-law has flown over from Canada. We're taking turns in keeping watch."

He felt like asking:

"What's that got to do with me?"

Hortense was Jeanne's sister, not his. He scarcely knew her, for they seldom met. He liked Bernard Bertaut, the husband, but only as a distant acquaintance.

"If I'm bothering you now, it's in order to ask you to come early. It would be better if you got here before the crowd, like the other members of the family."

"At what time?"

"Nine o'clock at the latest. The funeral Mass is at ten. There'll be a big crowd. After the funeral there'll be a lunch at the Hôtel de la Couronne for the family and close friends."

She asked him no questions about Alice. She did not even mention the girl's name, merely saying:

"Are you being well looked after? Have you got everything you want?"

"Everything's all right."

"See you tomorrow. Be sure to come in good time."

He knew the house, just outside the town, close to the workshop, which was built of reddish brick. It was huge but lacked light and gaiety even on the sunniest days.

"That was my wife," he felt impelled to announce to Alice.

The girl looked up from her plate and merely asked: "Is she all right?"

"I suppose so. I didn't ask her."

He finished his meal and while she was clearing up he went to watch television, taking his glass of wine with him.

And now the last evening had come. He wanted it to be an exceptional one, which he could remember if their relations, later on, became less frequent and less intimate.

He followed her upstairs, feeling the need to repeat the same gestures as though to reassure himself.

"I'll have to leave at half past seven tomorrow."

"Are you taking the deaf-mute?"

"No. He'll go to the mussel beds by himself. He'll have to go there on foot and just see to the cleaning of the shells, because he's not allowed to drive."

By now, she undressed in front of him as if she had done so all her life. She no longer asked him to put out the light. There were certain little gestures to which he had grown accustomed, which had become familiar to him, as when she cleaned her teeth and then brushed her hair.

She displayed no eagerness. They were going to make love: so what? Weren't thousands of couples making love at that very moment?

He, on the contrary, wanted it to remain something exceptional, to be somehow different. She got into bed, and without switching off the light he lay down beside her.

"Tell me, Alice, are you beginning to be a little bit fond of me?"

How many times he had asked her that question!

She appeared to think it over, then replied frankly:

"I don't know."

"During the day, do you ever think about me?"

"I don't have much time to."

"Do people in shops ask you any questions?"

"No. They look at me as if I were something peculiar. When I go out I hear the old women start to whisper."

"We mustn't let things change between us when my wife comes back. It matters a great deal to me. I'd never loved anybody before. I didn't know what it was. Now I shouldn't be able to do without you."

And as she remained silent, gazing up at the ceiling:

"What are you thinking about?"

"About what you said."

"What d'you think of it?"

"I don't know how you're proposing to manage. After all, she's your wife."

"I could get a divorce."

"On what grounds? D'you think she'd agree to a divorce?"

He knew she would not. Jeanne had principles. She was Mme Lecoin and she would remain Mme Lecoin until her death.

"Perhaps someday we'll go away together."

He was reverting to his obsession. Go away where?

147

Wasn't he too deeply rooted in Marsilly to settle down anywhere else? Wouldn't he miss it all, the house, the mussel beds where he spent hours every morning, his call at Mimile's and then, in the afternoon, his expeditions to the station at La Rochelle?

He was conscious that all his projects were unrealizable, but he wanted to believe that somehow or other he would manage not to lose Alice.

"Would it make a difference to you if I didn't come up here every day?"

"Maybe."

She did not say a straightforward yes. He could not understand her. There were times when he felt her close to him and a few minutes later she seemed remote and indifferent.

He took her more passionately than usual, with a sort of frenzy, and he read a look of fear in her eyes.

This time he did not withdraw. He didn't care if he made her pregnant. It would be his child, their child, and Jeanne would just have to accept it in the house.

Surprised, she asked him:

"What were you doing?"

And he replied, forthrightly:

"Making love."

"Aren't you afraid of getting me pregnant?"

"And what of it? I should be happy to have a child by you."

She was stupefied. If he did not understand her, neither did she understand him. He lay stretched out on

148

his back, as was now his custom. The difference was that now he could see her in the light.

He felt the need to talk to her, without knowing exactly about what, in order to keep in touch with her.

"One day you must tell me about your life."

"There's nothing to tell. In charity institutions one day's just like another."

"Were they very strict with you?"

"They weren't men. They were nuns."

"Did you have to go to Mass?"

"Every morning. We got up at six and we had ten minutes to dress in."

"Did you have a room to yourself?"

"There were six of us together, in each of the rooms."

"Did you have friends?"

"Just schoolfellows. After Mass, we were allowed a bowl of coffee and some bread. Then there were two hours of lessons. The nuns insisted on our writing neatly.

"And they wanted us to be very good at sewing, too. We used to make bags, which they sold. We washed all the laundry outside, even in winter, without coats on."

She was not complaining. She was stating the facts.

"Were you glad to leave?"

"Yes."

He did not want to remind her of Paquot.

"So really, before you came here you hadn't lived at all."

"Well, I'm sixteen years old."

"Why do you go to Mass on Sundays?"

"Out of habit. Where I was, the chapel wasn't heated. We had to go to confession and take communion once a week."

He, too, had had to go to church when he was very young, but only on Sundays.

By the time he was thirteen he had been free to do what he liked, apart from his work on the farm. But the work went on from sunrise to sunset. Ten times a day he could hear the shrill voice of the farmer's wife, standing in the yard with her arms akimbo, calling: "Victor!"

Wherever he was he had to hurry up, for she was the boss, not her fool of a husband.

"Go get the ladder and climb up to get me a couple of squabs."

There were geese and ducks in the barnyard, too. On Saturday evenings she went off to sell her eggs and poultry at the market, and he had a brief respite.

Surely both he and Alice had to make up for the childhood they had missed! He had grown tough. He had become the Chief, *le patron.*

And now, at forty-five, he was proving as vulnerable as a very young man, and his whole fate, for good or ill, was in the hands of a chit of a girl.

"Do I seem old to you?"

"I don't know how old you are."

"Forty-five."

"Your wife's older than you are, isn't she?"

"Three years."

"She seems a lot older."

"Probably because her hair is gray."

She had not given him a direct answer; she was often like that, as evasive as an eel.

"If I were free would you be willing to marry me?"

She remained silent for a long while, and this hurt him.

"But you're not free."

"Suppose I should become free."

"We could decide things then."

"Wouldn't you like to live with me properly, as man and wife?"

"I don't know."

It was her usual reply when he pressed her a little.

"You're not really fond of me, are you?"

"I don't know you very well yet."

"And yet," he said unhappily, "I may perhaps have got you pregnant."

"That's got nothing to do with it."

He wondered if she was really irresponsible. In a few minutes she would be in his arms again.

"You know practically everything about me," he objected. "I've told you about my youth, about my early days."

"Yes."

"What else d'you want to know?"

And she repeated, yet again: "I don't know."

Jeanne read him like a book, as the saying is, and had done so from the first moment of their acquaintance. Might she not sometimes be mistaken? He often resented her clear-sightedness. She seemed to him like a mother who was sometimes indulgent, at other times cold and reserved.

She had not mentioned Alice over the telephone. And yet she must have thought about the girl, and he was sure that she suspected what had happened. What she probably did not know was that he was deeply and irrevocably in love.

Was she not afraid that someone else might take her place? Or had she too much self-confidence for that?

He made love to the girl once more, and this time when he came she was not taken by surprise.

"It feels all hot," she said.

"D'you know what I'd like to ask you?"

"No."

"To let me spend the night here with you. It's probably the last chance we'll have for a long time."

"The bed's not wide."

"That doesn't matter. We'd be sleeping together."

She seemed to think it over, weighing the pros and cons. She must have begun to realize her power over him, and she might be playing a game.

"If you really want to."

He went to turn off the light and she asked:

"Can't I put on my nightgown again?"

"I'd rather you didn't."

"Shan't we be cold?"

"Not together. Come."

He drew her toward him and laid her head against his chest.

"Are you all right?"

"Yes."

She added after a moment, pushing back the hair that was hanging over her face:

"You've got a man's smell."

She sighed, and almost immediately began to grow drowsy. She kept moving her arm about, not knowing where to put it.

"Good night, dearest."

It was the first time he had called her that. She answered in a faint voice that already seemed to come from far away:

"Good night."

Her breathing became deeper and more regular. He felt her whole body against him, and this moved him so much that his eyes filled with tears.

Why did Jeanne have to come back tomorrow? He felt it was unfair that he should be obliged to live with her. Just because one day, over twenty years ago, he had danced with her, because he had thought she would make him a useful wife, he was now denied the right to love whom he chose.

The whole village was against him. He understood the glances that were cast at him and he could imagine the women's gossip.

"He ought to be ashamed of running after a slip of a

girl! And how can she let him do it, a man of his age? He just takes advantage of other people's misfortunes. If his sister-in-law hadn't died and his wife hadn't had to go to Cholet . . ."

Théo, meanwhile, merely went on sneering. They all seemed to be waiting for something to happen. But what?

For years he had been the strong man, the Chief, the rich man of the neighborhood, and nobody questioned his superiority.

And now that a slip of a girl could twist him around her finger, he had come down from his pedestal. Not only had he become a commonplace fellow, but he was more vulnerable than anyone else in the village and he was making himself ridiculous.

Alice moved her head. Lecoin's chest was hard, and presently she slipped over onto her pillow without wakening.

He would have liked that night to last forever. He was not sleepy. He lay thinking. He did not choose his thoughts. They reverted constantly to his wife's pale face and her almost masculine figure.

He refused to be depressed. He was sure it could all be worked out. At all costs, it must be worked out.

If Jeanne dismissed Alice from the house he would refuse to stay there.

Of course he could set her up in a little apartment in La Rochelle and go to visit her every day. But it wouldn't be the same thing. He needed to have her there all day and all night, to look at her and talk to her.

She was sleeping soundly by his side, pouting like a small girl.

He thought and thought. He became exhausted from constantly envisaging the same problem and eventually he fell asleep. Twice during the night he woke up; each time he felt the bed beside him to make sure that she was there.

At last he heard a slight noise. She had crept out of bed cautiously and was dressing in the darkness.

She opened the door and went downstairs, where, as on any other day, she prepared the coffee.

It was morning, but there were still nearly two hours to go before sunrise.

He put on his pajamas, dressing gown, and slippers and went down. His hair was tousled, and so was hers. Neither of them had had time to wash, and this increased the sense of intimacy.

"Did you sleep well?"

"Yes. I don't think I woke up once all night."

"You fell asleep with your head on my chest and you lay like that for a long time."

"Would you like your eggs now?"

"No. When I come down again. I'll just have a cup of coffee."

He drank it in the kitchen, while he watched her coming and going. He felt nervous. He would have liked a glass of wine to calm his shaking hands, but he dared not, so early in the morning, in front of her.

He took a long bath and in his mind's eye once more saw Alice bathing in the washtub. Then he shaved very closely, as he usually did on Sundays, when he had time to devote to his toilet.

He had a black suit that was rather tight, for he had had it made almost ten years earlier for a wedding and he practically never wore it. He had a hat, too, dating from the same period, for usually he wore his seaman's cap.

A bright sun had risen and a few luminous white clouds were scudding across the sky.

He went down, feeling awkward in his Sunday clothes, and entered the kitchen. This time he poured himself a glass of wine.

"Are you going to be home for dinner?"

"Yes, a little late."

He held out his arms to her. She came to him, without enthusiasm. It was always like that during the daytime.

"It'll be all right!" he whispered in her ear.

Then he kissed her slowly and very tenderly.

"Till tonight, Alice."

"Till tonight."

The deaf-mute opened the door of the car and Victor waved good-by to him.

He took the Niort road. It was the best, though not the shortest. He drove through the villages of the Vendée, with their low houses, and automatically cast a professional glance at the cattle in the meadows. Everything around him was flat, and the sky seemed immense, with virtually no visible horizon line.

He drove through Les Essarts and Mortagne, and the milestones began to mention Cholet. The nearer he got to it the more his heart sank.

A few minutes before nine o'clock he drew up not far from his brother-in-law's house. The door was draped with black crape dotted with silver tears, and surmounted by the letter B in a shield. Passers-by stopped for a moment before proceeding on their way.

He went in and was met by a smell of wax candles and chrysanthemums.

The door of the living room on the right was open, and the room had been turned into a mortuary chamber. The coffin was already closed, and he took a sprig of box, dipped it in holy water, and traced a cross in the air.

A girl came up to him, noiselessly, while he was pretending to pray. It was one of his nieces, Albertine or Joséfa, he never knew which. The fact was that he saw the Bertauts so seldom.

"Your wife must be in the dining room."

He kissed her cheek, muttering condolences. In the dining room there were about a dozen people, some of whom he did not know; Jeanne performed the introductions. Everyone was dressed in black. Everyone wore an expression suitable to the occasion.

"Would you like to wash?" Jeanne asked him.

"I don't need to."

157

"Are you thirsty?"

There were two bottles of wine and some glasses on a tray and he poured himself a drink.

He felt ill at ease. Jeanne was grateful to him for having come early, as she had asked him to. Some people were sitting, others remained standing. One man, whose name he had not caught, was smoking a cigar.

"It's better for her than having to go on suffering much longer."

The husband seemed lost, as though he did not know what to cling to. He was one of those who were standing. Lecoin was close behind him, and Bernard sighed:

"It's terrible. It feels as if everything had collapsed."

Several people were talking at once in low voices.

"She was such a cheerful soul. During the war she kept everybody going."

A priest appeared in the room for a moment, clasped several hands and muttered unintelligible words, then disappeared.

There were signs of bustle in the street. People went into the mortuary chamber, made the sign of the cross, their lips moving in prayer, and then went out to stand on the opposite sidewalk.

He saw two nuns who remained kneeling somewhat longer.

"Perhaps someone should go and relieve Albertine?"

An old lady whom he did not know offered her services.

"Another glass?" the widower said to Lecoin. He

158

drank one, too; he must have been drinking since early morning, for his breath was already thick. He was a good fellow, red-faced and tubby, a habitual *bon vivant* who had suddenly found himself all at sea.

At intervals somebody went to cast a look into the street.

"The staff are here already."

There were some forty of them, men and women, chiefly women, for Bernard specialized in the hand-hemmed handkerchiefs for which Cholet was famous.

From time to time Victor felt Jeanne's eyes fixed on him. She looked grave, but her face betrayed no other feeling.

"The priest and the choirboy are here."

Then came the hearse. Everyone got ready to go out. The coffin had been placed on a stretcher and covered with a black cloth. It was lifted onto the hearse.

The church was less than three hundred yards away and no cars had been provided.

The mourners formed a procession of a sort, after some hesitation, as each of them tried to find his right place.

On the sidewalks, people stopped and took off their hats. Victor and his wife were up front, with the close relatives. Sheaves of flowers and wreaths were piled onto the hearse, and when they reached the square in front of the church the bells began to ring. People were already sitting in the bays. The organ was booming. The priest went into the sacristy, followed by the choirboy.

Victor was in the second row now, near the bier, and vague thoughts suggested by the atmosphere passed through his mind. A human being, his sister-in-law, whom he had so often seen laughing, was there in a wooden box, and very soon would be laid in the earth for ever.

And what if, instead of Hortense, it had been Jeanne? He could not help thinking of that. In the past five years Jeanne had had two thromboses. The doctor had not concealed from Victor that a third might prove fatal. He had given her some small pink tablets, a bottle of which she always carried in her bag.

He saw the side of her face, her heavy jaw, her steady gaze fixed on the altar.

The choirboy rang his bell and the Mass began, while in the rood loft the choir intoned the ritual chant.

Lecoin felt ill at ease. The smell of the flowers close by him mingled with that of the candles, and against his will his eyes reverted continually to his wife's face.

Right now Alice must be doing the marketing in the almost deserted streets of Marsilly. That evening he would not go up to the second floor to sleep beside her. He thought he could still feel her head against his breast and hear her regular breathing.

This was not the moment to think of anything further. What plans could he make? In fact, he was dependent on that hard-featured woman sitting in the front row.

She must have guessed what had happened. Would she

speak to him about it on the way home or would she pretend to suspect nothing? He felt hot. He was not used to wearing a collar and tie. At the Offertory he followed the rest. Scores of people could be heard shuffling on the paving stones, and each of them knelt down in turn to kiss the paten and then put alms into the collection bowl.

Then came the Absolution, and the church door was flung open wide and suddenly let in the sunlight.

The coffin was being carried again. The procession reformed and moved toward the graveyard.

Here, too, those people who had been unable to get to the church were waiting. Bernard was an important person, and the Mayor and several municipal councilors had come.

Lecoin looked at the hole into which the coffin was being lowered; then he involuntarily glanced at his wife and as quickly looked away, ashamed of his thoughts.

Wouldn't that have settled everything? He bore Jeanne no resentment. She was not to blame. But who, in fact, was to blame? Surely it was he himself, who had married her?

But could he, at twenty-five, have foreseen that twenty years later he would fall madly in love?

He would go away with Alice. At that moment, standing there in the cemetery, his mind was made up. He would leave half his money and his land to Jeanne, for the estate was held jointly.

He was convinced she would not be unhappy. On the

161

contrary. She would run the business, as she already did to an extent, and she could take on someone to go to the mussel beds with the deaf-mute.

His mind was confused. People were shaking hands once more. The sun was high in the sky. Little by little the mourners scattered, sometimes threading their way between the graves.

"You don't look quite yourself."

This from Jeanne, who had come up beside him.

"I'm too hot. The ceremony was so long."

He felt as if he had been caught red-handed.

"We're all going to lunch at the restaurant. There's a room reserved at the Hôtel de la Couronne."

They went there on foot, in small groups following one another at a short distance. The manager of the hotel stood on the front step to receive them. A table was set for some twenty people, and glasses and bottles of apéritif stood on a sideboard.

"What will you have, monsieur?"

He looked at the labels on the bottles and decided on a glass of port. He drank it avidly and promptly helped himself again.

Everyone was drinking. They dared not clink glasses. To whose health could they have drunk?

Bernard was mopping his brow and the thick nape of his neck, which bulged over his collar.

"You're lucky, Victor. Jeanne's health is good. You can't imagine what it's like to be suddenly left alone. My

162

youngest girl is getting married and I shall be all by my-self at home."

His eyes grew moist. He, too, poured himself a drink. There was a murmur of voices and the headwaiter came at last to announce that lunch was served.

He was placed at some distance from Jeanne, beside the youngest daughter of the family, the one of whose engagement he had just been told.

He looked at the dining room around him, the walls paneled in wood from top to bottom and the huge chandelier, lighted in broad daylight.

Wasn't this the room they used for engagement parties and weddings as well as funerals? And was not the menu more or less the same for all these occasions?

Lobster mousse was followed by duck with orange, and finally a *bombe glacée.*

There were at least three kinds of wine, and the wine waiter never left their glasses empty, so that voices grew louder and louder all around the table. Some people probably forgot why they were gathered there.

"Are you going home tonight?" his neighbor asked.

"Yes. I have to be at the mussel beds tomorrow."

"Does my aunt go with you?"

"No. Some women do, but Jeanne works in the office, takes orders, and sees to the invoices and consignments."

"She must be invaluable to you."

He replied, to his own surprise: "Yes."

And it was true that the work Jeanne did was some-

163

thing he could not have undertaken. He had not thought of that.

Cigars were handed around, as after a feast, and some men pocketed theirs to smoke later. Faces were flushed, and brandy was served with the coffee.

That night Victor would have to sleep on the first floor, in the same bed as . . .

He could not bear the thought of it. Why, in God's name, since there was no shared feeling between them? He looked at her across the table and met her eyes, which were fixed on his.

She usually guessed everything. Could she guess what he was thinking at that moment, what he had been thinking during the Absolution?

Some of the guests rose to leave and went to shake hands with Bernard, who got up from his chair each time. Soon only the immediate family were left at the table, and Lecoin made a sign to his wife. She nodded in reply, and there followed a round of handshakes and embraces.

"Where did you leave the car?"

"Just about opposite the house."

"I'll have to go in and get my suitcase."

They walked side by side along the sunlit sidewalk, casting their lengthened shadows in front of them.

Why did Lecoin feel as if it were Sunday? Probably because of the way he was dressed. Moreoever, he was unaccustomed to walking with his wife along a sidewalk.

The streets seemed almost empty. They crossed the center of the town.

When they got to the car Jeanne went inside the house and presently reappeared with an old woman who closed the door behind her. The black hangings had vanished. Life was resuming its normal course.

It was Jeanne who spoke first, while they were passing through a small village where children were playing in front of a house.

"I hope you took precautions, at least?"

Caught unawares, he did not know what to reply, and merely mumbled:

"What precautions?"

"Don't act simple, Victor."

She was not angry. Her voice was not harsh. On the contrary, she seemed almost to be taking him under her protection.

"I don't mind your making love together but I don't want to see you in jail."

"You needn't worry."

"Did she look after you all right?"

"Very well."

"Can she cook a little?"

"I suppose they taught her that in the home she was in. They taught her to sew too."

Why did he go into these details about her?

"It was run by nuns," he added.

"She didn't go to Mass on Sunday."

"She's stopped going."

"I hope you didn't do it in our bedroom?"

"No."

"In hers?"

"Yes."

He was unbelievably uncomfortable. He felt as if his wife was degrading his wonderful love by reducing it to a mere act, a matter of purely physical attraction.

He wanted to shout: "But I love her, don't you understand? If you want to stay in our bedroom, all right, but I shall go and sleep with her."

He could not quite conceal his distress.

"God knows you've had plenty of adventures," she said, "but this is the first time I've seen you in this state."

"What do you mean?"

"Are you in love, Victor?"

"No."

He hated saying that, and mentally begged Alice's forgiveness for it. What else could he have replied?

"Have the local people noticed?"

"Noticed what?"

"Your relations. You don't seem to understand what I'm telling you. There are some things that aren't hard to guess, when one knows you. And the gossips aren't going to wait for you to walk about arm in arm with her to understand.

"Not to mention the deaf-mute, who always knows everything. In his eyes you can do no wrong."

Lecoin felt his unease increasing. She made everything seem petty. He realized that henceforward his love affair would consist of furtive embraces. Knowing Alice, he foresaw that she would always have her eyes fixed on the door.

For her, Jeanne was the mistress of the house, and she respected her.

"Well! It'll pass off just as it began."

He was boiling inwardly, but tried not to betray it.

"Look what speed you're driving at!"

He was going at over eighty-five miles an hour without noticing it.

"I'm thirsty," he grumbled as they came to a village.

He stopped before a small café with a blue-painted front.

"Are you coming in too?"

"No. Don't forget you've got to drive."

He shrugged his shoulders. For the first time in their married life he felt rebellious, and as she spoke he actually hated her.

A girl was standing behind the counter in the small, empty room.

"Have you any good brandy?"

She showed him a bottle on the shelf.

"I've got this one."

"Give me a large glass of it."

"A double?"

"Yes, a double."

His hands were shaking with nervous irritation.

"Another, please."

He felt ashamed of drinking like this when a young girl was serving him.

"Another double?"

"Yes."

He felt for the money in his pocket, and finished his drink more slowly. Jeanne, in the car, was staring straight ahead, and as she sat there calm and rather stiff she really looked as if it all belonged to her.

"Thanks, mademoiselle."

"Have you been drinking brandy?"

"Yes."

"How many? Two, three, four?"

He shrugged his shoulders without answering. Three quarters of an hour later they caught sight of the houses on the outskirts of Marsilly and the sea shimmering, on their right, under the setting sun.

CHAPTER 7

When he drove through the front gate, Jeanne had already taken her key out of her handbag, and he stopped for a moment at the foot of the stoop to allow her to get out.

Then he drove into the garage, and was somewhat surprised to see no sign of the deaf-mute, who usually, when he came home, emerged from somewhere or other as though scenting his arrival.

When he went into the house his wife had not yet taken off her coat and hat. She was coming out of the kitchen.

"It's odd. Alice isn't downstairs."

His immediate thought was that she must have taken

advantage of his absence to run away, and his expression must have betrayed it.

"She may be upstairs," muttered Jeanne.

"What would she be doing there at this time of day?"

There was nothing cooking on the stove, not a saucepan, not even the kettle. He rushed upstairs four steps at a time and looked into the bedroom, which, as he had expected, was empty. The bed, which had not been used on the previous night, was smoothly made; as he went past the wardrobe mirror he saw himself looking haggard.

He went up to the second floor, opened the door of Alice's room, and halted, his heart in his mouth. Did he really scream? He felt as though he had uttered a wild scream as he rushed forward, but he stopped short before the bed where Alice lay, dressed in her checked apron. Her staring eyes were glassy, her mouth was open and her tongue hanging out. Her skin had already turned bluish.

"My poor Victor, keep calm."

His wife had followed him and stood on the threshold, seeming to fill up the whole doorway.

Almost timidly, he touched a hand hanging down from the bed, and it was cold and lifeless. He could not look at those unseeing eyes whose fixed stare terrified him. He bent forward and, with an effort, closed her lids.

"Don't touch anything, Victor. It's the police who . . ."

He did not understand. He understood nothing. He

was dumfounded. There was not even any sign of disorder in the little room.

"It's not possible."

His voice was choking. He shed no tears. His dismay was too great. He seemed almost stunned.

"Have you seen Doudou about?"

"No."

He would have liked to tell her that she was mistaken, that Doudou was incapable of such a deed. On the girl's neck there were some dark marks. Someone had strangled her. Inevitably, he thought of Doudou's enormous hands.

"I'll call up the police."

She went downstairs. The police station was only two hundred yards away. He did not know what to do or where to go.

He was still there, leaning against the frame of the door, when he heard steps on the stair. Jeanne came in, followed by Sergeant Cornu, who was an old friend.

The sergeant was shocked, too.

"When did you discover her?"

"A few minutes ago, when we came home."

Jeanne was speaking, for he would have been incapable of doing so.

"We'd come back from my sister's funeral at Cholet. We were surprised not to see her in the kitchen. My husband went upstairs. I had a sudden foreboding and I followed him.

"I called up Dr. Bourseau. He'll be here very soon."

171

"And I must let them know at La Rochelle. The Chief will want to come and see for himself."

Lecoin did not have the courage to be alone with the body once more. He followed them downstairs. Everything seemed quite unreal to him. His legs felt weak and he would readily have lain down on the ground.

It all seemed so impossible! He recalled last night, the one, the only one, they had spent together. She had fallen asleep against his chest and he had ended by breathing to the rhythm of her breath.

He loved her. He wanted to howl it out. As far as Jeanne was concerned it was pointless, for she had already understood and was looking at him with surprise mingled with pity.

She knew, of course, that he had taken advantage of her absence to make love with Alice, but she had never imagined so violent a passion.

She went herself to pour a glass of brandy and then hand it to him. He drank it mechanically, forgetting to thank her.

"Sergeant Cornu here, from Marsilly. I've got to speak to the Chief."

"Is it all that important?"

"Yes."

Someone opened the door; it was Dr. Bourseau, who had been sent for from Mimile's, where he had been playing cards.

"What's happening, my dears?"

"Alice is dead."

This time it was Victor who spoke, in a hoarse voice. He led the doctor up the stairs and stopped in front of the door on the second floor, which had been left open.

He almost expected to find Alice peacefully asleep. It didn't seem possible that anyone . . .

"Were her eyes closed?" the doctor asked in some surprise.

"No. I closed them."

Bourseau grasped her hand as though to feel for the pulse. At the same time he examined the bruises on her throat.

"It's over an hour, an hour and a half maybe, since she was strangled," he muttered. "Have you told the police?"

"Yes. The sergeant is downstairs. He's calling up his Chief at La Rochelle."

"Where were you this afternoon?"

"At Cholet. My wife had been there since Sunday, because her sister was dying of cancer. The funeral took place today and I went to it. I left this morning early and we've just got back."

He was not even conscious that he was speaking. He suddenly remembered Doudou's hut and he ran downstairs, hurried out, and strode toward the hut. It was empty.

The doctor had come downstairs too and was waiting for the inspector. Victor asked him:

"Did you see the deaf-mute when you were in the café?"

173

"He looked in about half an hour ago or more. He was looking for someone."

"For whom?"

"He couldn't tell us, of course, but he stared at each of us in turn and even went to have a look in the kitchen."

The inspector appeared next, accompanied by a constable.

"Who is it that's been killed?"

"The maid. She's upstairs, lying on her bed. She's been strangled."

Inspector Dartois was about to go up when a light step was heard on the stoop and to everyone's surprise Doudou appeared, seeming astonished himself at seeing so many people.

He immediately looked toward Lecoin, with a troubled expression, as if humbly begging forgiveness.

Everyone else stood motionless, impressed by the deaf-mute's attitude. He was barefoot as usual and bareheaded, and he was staring at his two hands.

Then he began to express himself with gestures. Only Lecoin understood him. To begin with he pointed to his mouth and uttered a peculiar snigger; he raised one hand to shoulder level as though to represent someone very short.

Théo. There was no possible doubt about it.

Then he pointed to the ceiling, to indicate the upper floors.

Lecoin interpreted, for the inspector's benefit:

"Théo Porchet came in my absence and went up to the second floor."

Doudou, who was lip-reading, shook his head to show that this was not quite accurate. He pointed to the kitchen and sketched a woman's figure in the air. Then he lifted two fingers and once more pointed to the stairs.

Lecoin stiffened. In a low, scarcely audible voice he stammered:

"They went up together."

"The girl and the hardware dealer?"

He nodded.

Now Doudou's finger pointed to the courtyard, and finally he struck his own chest. He had seen through the window.

He went on miming, and Lecoin interpreting.

"He saw them through the window. He came into the house and went upstairs without making a noise. He never makes a noise."

The increasingly complicated gestures conveyed nothing to the rest, who all looked at Victor.

"He found them together . . ."

A great gasp broke from him and he had barely time to go over to the wall and lean against it, hiding his face, before bursting into sobs.

Everyone was silent. It was frightening to see this powerful and self-confident man crying like a child. Nobody moved. Nobody tried to comfort him or lay a friendly hand on his shoulder, for each of them, Jeanne above all, realized that it would be useless.

As for the deaf-mute's face, it expressed utter confusion. He understood nothing. He had done what he felt it his duty to do.

When Lecoin turned around at last, wiping his cheeks with his cuff, Jeanne offered him a glass which he thrust away with the back of his hand and sent crashing to the floor.

CHAPTER 8

Nobody stirred, and total silence reigned in the house. Turning to his servant, and articulating the syllables very clearly so as to make himself understood, Lecoin managed to ask:

"Why did you strangle her?"

As he spoke he could not help looking at the deaf-mute's enormous hands.

The latter seemed surprised, as though he did not expect such a reproach.

He was obviously distressed, and tried hard to explain himself. First he pointed to Lecoin, then he once more

177

sketched a woman's figure in the air and pretended to clasp her in his arms.

"He says I loved her."

Doudou nodded assent. What did it matter now whether other people knew it? And had not Victor been the first to give himself away?

He said to his wife:

"Give me a drink after all."

He was swaying, clearly at the end of his strength.

"And you, Doctor?"

"Thanks."

They were in the dining room, in a domestic setting where everything was orderly and spotless. The open door gave a glimpse of the kitchen and, through the kitchen window, of the courtyard, where a little sunlight still lingered.

She offered to pour the inspector a glass, but he shook his head. As for Sergeant Cornu, who at first had produced a thick notebook and pencil from his pocket, he had given up taking notes.

"And then, Doudou?" asked Lecoin.

The deaf-mute did not clearly understand the question. For him, it was all so natural. With a telling gesture, he depicted two people making love.

This time Victor did not need to interpret.

Once again Doudou pointed to the kitchen, then to the ceiling. Didn't this mean that in his eyes it was the girl who was guilty of treachery? The man might have been anyone.

She was the one Lecoin loved, and she ought to have made him happy. But he had scarcely been out of the house for a day when she betrayed him with Théo.

The latter had not even tried to protect her. Doudou mimed the scene: while he was strangling the girl, the hardware dealer had fled.

Then, waving his arms, he showed how he had hunted far and wide for Théo, and his hands clutched an invisible throat.

He had gone to Mimile's in search of Théo, and had even looked in the kitchen there.

He had not found him. Porchet must have gone into hiding somewhere, in terror.

With outspread arms and open hands, Doudou seemed to be saying:

"There, that's all."

Then he looked at his master with great tears in his lashless eyes.

There was a long silence. The sergeant broke it at last.

"Shall I handcuff him, Inspector?"

The latter shrugged his shoulders as though to say he didn't care. Doudou showed no desire to escape. He stood there hanging his head, trying to understand.

When the sergeant fastened the handcuffs, which were scarcely big enough to encircle his wrists, he merely jerked his hands apart and the chain broke.

He was shaking his head, while his hands sketched a gesture of flight. He was not going to run away. There was no need to chain him up like an animal.

"What shall I do, Chief?"

"Nothing. Stay with him till I come down again."

Lecoin followed the inspector upstairs. So did Dr. Bourseau.

Once they were in the room, the doctor commented: "There's no point now in my explaining things."

He went up to the bed and lifted the girl's apron. She was wearing nothing underneath it.

"I bet it was the deaf-mute who covered her legs."

Lecoin looked at the washtub in the corner, in which, two days before, Alice had crouched in the soapy water.

"What'll you do with her?" asked the doctor.

"I've got to have her taken to the morgue for the autopsy."

Victor gave a start. That word evoked images that hurt him more than if the scalpel had been thrust into his own body.

"Is it necessary?" he asked.

"It's essential. Especially since the confession of guilt has only been made in the form of gestures. Doesn't he know the deaf-and-dumb language?"

"No. He's never left the village except to go to La Rochelle with me."

He was unable to feel any resentment against Doudou. Perhaps in his place, under the shock of such a discovery, he would have acted in the same way.

He bore no resentment toward Alice either. He remembered her silences, the inertness of her body when he sought to kiss her during the daytime.

She did not know what love meant.

"Now I must inform the magistrate."

The three of them went downstairs again. The inspector gave orders for Doudou to be taken to the police car, a small gray car in which a constable was waiting at the wheel.

"Hello . . . Yes, sir . . . Inspector Dartois here . . . I've got a murder to report from Marsilly . . . It's at the home of Victor Lecoin, who owns the mussel beds . . . No, he's not involved . . . We've got the guilty man, a deaf-mute who appears to be mentally subnormal. . . ."

Doudou let them take him away like a dog whose masters have cast him off, and to the end he kept his face turned toward Lecoin.

He was asking to be forgiven, though he did not quite know for what. There were some things beyond his understanding.

Jeanne was busy filling glasses. She did not neglect her duties as mistress of the house. It was from her office that the inspector had telephoned, that office where next morning she would resume her seat, just as, that night, she would resume her place in the double bed.

Some interested spectators had gathered in the road, outside the gate.

"The public prosecutor, the examining magistrate, and the clerk will be here soon. I'll wait for them, but I'm sending the car on. You go with it, sergeant, and keep an eye on the deaf-mute."

"He won't stir," muttered Lecoin.

"I've got to obey the regulations. Tomorrow morning I must ask you to call at my office, where he'll have to repeat his statement, if we can call it that. You'll have to interpret his gestures once again so that the report can be drawn up."

"Do you think he'll be sentenced?"

"No. But he'll probably be shut up in a mental home for the rest of his days. He's become a danger to the public. He admits himself that he pursued the man you call Théo to deal with him in the same way."

It was only next morning that they learned, through local gossip, that the hardware dealer had spent the rest of that afternoon and part of the night in a dark corner of his attic.

He was not seen at Mimile's for several days, and he did not appear in his shop either.

"He's not well," was his wife's reply to all inquiries.

At eight o'clock that evening Alice's body was taken away in an ambulance. Lecoin had shut himself up, alone, in the living room and watched through the net curtains.

He had dreamed up so many projects! And not one of them would ever be realized. Alice had told him as much. But then Alice had not been in love. He had been, he still was the only one in love.

He remembered certain troubling thoughts that had beset him that morning while he gazed at the bier.

It was Alice who had gone. It was Jeanne who was left,

and who, at that very moment, with perfect self-control, was relating the course of events to the members of the judiciary.

Silently, because he wanted to see no one, he went upstairs once more to the second floor. The bed still retained the imprint of the girl's thin body.

Down below, the officials finally departed. Only a few curious spectators still lingered by the roadside.

He went slowly downstairs.

Now there were only two of them in the house.

And tomorrow Jeanne, if he knew her, would go off first thing in the morning in search of a maid-of-all-work and a man.

It was all over. Life would never be the same again. Lecoin felt that something had died within him. No! He was determined, all the same, to keep a tiny flame secretly alive, deep within his heart.

He refused to eat, but he drank some brandy right from the bottle, staring defiantly at Jeanne.

Épalinges, March 9, 1970